Religious Consolation

SALZWASSER
VERLAG

Joseph Dowe

Religious Consolation

Reprint of the original, first published in 1863.

1st Edition 2022 | ISBN: 978-3-37500-174-2

Verlag (Publisher): Salzwasser Verlag GmbH, Zeilweg 44, 60439 Frankfurt, Deutschland
Vertretungsberechtigt (Authorized to represent): E. Roepke, Zeilweg 44, 60439 Frankfurt, Deutschland
Druck (Print): Books on Demand GmbH, In de Tarpen 42, 22848 Norderstedt, Deutschland

RELIGIOUS

CONSOLATION

"Ye believe in God, believe also in me. . . . . . I go to prepare a place for you; . . . . . that where I am, there ye may be also."
JOHN xiv. 1-3.

A NEW EDITION.

BOSTON

1863.

CONTENTS.

INTRODUCTION.

CHRISTIAN FAITH.

"Ye believe in God, believe also in me."

The end of human existence on earth is improvement, moral growth, progress towards spiritual perfection. Trouble, as one of the means conducive to this end, is an essential part of the system under which we live. It is therefore a manifestation of divine beneficence, a proof of the interest that the Father takes in us, not a ground of complaint or distrust. The question which we need to solve is this,—how can the outward trouble be so received that it shall not disturb the feelings which we carry within us—how shall the mirror of the breast be saved from reflecting the images of disaster? To this question Jesus has pointed out the only answer in those memorable words which he addressed to his disciples in view of his separation from them: "Let not your heart be troubled: ye believe in God, believe also in me." Christian faith it is which will enable us to preserve serenity amidst all changes of condition. We may be patient and calm, even more, may be thoughtful of improvement, and successful in its acquisition, whilst the severest calamities are proving their own impotency and our strength, if we have this safeguard and solace. Christian faith can sustain us, comfort us, guide us, when every thing else would be ineffectual for either of these purposes, and might only aggravate our distress. Let this faith abide in the soul, and no acquaintance with disappointment can render it distrustful or perverse. The Christian believes, therefore he is tranquil, submissive, steadfast in duty, therefore he makes progress when other men are thrown back, therefore his character, like the stars seen in the high latitudes of the earth, shines brightest over a scene of desolation.

This faith is indispensable to man's relief. He cannot do without it. His heart will be troubled, tempest-tost, overwhelmed, if he have it not. What can take its place? What can anticipate its offices of support and comfort? Sympathy may proffer its condolence, and soften the pangs over which it grieves; but it can neither heal the wounded affections nor revive the, down-stricken hopes. Philosophy may repeat its maxims drawn from long observation of life, and utter the counsels of wisdom; but they fall on the heart like the boastings of health on a sick man's ear, who feels that they but remind him of his distemper. Even the world may intrude, and invite the troubled soul to forget its griefs among the excitements of business or society; but the invitation grates harshly on the sensibilities, and seems rather like insult than condolence. When external sources of alleviation thus evince their insufficiency, if the soul which has not learned the lessons of faith turns in upon itself, what does it find to give it peace? No habit of resignation, no temper of acquiescence, no confidence in a love more far-sighted than its own, no hope of a richer good which shall issue from the disappointment, as the more abundant stream from the earth in which it seemed to be lost. All within is sad, while all without is distasteful; and if the sentiment, whether of passionate sorrow or of sullen endurance, which occupies the heart, were expressed in words, it would probably vent itself in abuse of life and crimination of God. Such is man's need of faith.

But what is this faith, which can render the invaluable service that in time of trouble we shall in vain seek elsewhere? Our Master presents it under a two-fold aspect,—as faith in God, and faith in his Son.

Faith in God as the Supreme, Eternal, Perfect One, faith in his character and government, in his presence and love, in his purposes and his unchangeableness.

It is faith in the Creator, who has framed the worlds, and filled them with life; who has established the principles which regulate the movements of matter, and the experiences of mind; the Former of the body, by whom this curious and delicate structure was raised from the dust, and who has not only made it subject to change and decay, but has determined the causes which shall work its overthrow, so that not a pain can be felt, nor a vital function cease, but in obedience to laws which sustain the health and life of countless multitudes; the Author of the spirit, which he has endowed with all its fine faculties and marvellous sympathies, and has put into this frail body, that it may both enjoy much and suffer much, that it may learn much and do much, through the connection and the mutual dependence which thence arise. Faith views God as the infinitely wise Original of all that is seen or known or felt.

It also contemplates him as the Guardian of the universe which he has created—the God of providence; without whose knowledge and consent nothing happens—whether it be the eruption of a volcano that buries cities in an instantaneous grave, or the fall of a sparrow in its solitary flight—whether it be the occasion that gathers friends to rejoice in the hopes of kindred hearts, or the event that calls them to join their tears and their prayers in the house of mourning. The God of providence—there is great meaning in these words. They describe a presence and a power which have connection with every circumstance of life, and which keep the laws of the Creator in exercise and his purposes in fulfilment through all which men call vicissitude, accident, or mystery. They express the continual dependence of all creatures upon God, and indicate the confidence with which events may be submitted to his will. Such a confidence is the fruit of Christian faith.

This faith likewise recognises the moral government of God, acknowledging that in the providence which he maintains he is setting forth and enforcing a discipline suited to promote the end for which the moral creation received its endowments. To the Christian this truth is as a "lamp to his feet and a light to his path." It reconciles the contradictory, it explains the ambiguous. He sees a purpose, a righteous and gracious purpose in all that he suffers, and the disappointment of his hopes, no less than the attainment of his wishes, seems to him as a page on which the hand of infinite Wisdom has written lessons for his study. How true to him are those words:

> Each blessing to my soul more dear
> Because conferred by thee!

but equally true those other lines:

> He everywhere hath rule,
> And all things serve his might;
> His every act pure blessing is,
> His path unsullied light.

To be the subject of a government just in its principles, invariable in its administration, and beneficent in its results, should be, and by the Christian believer is, accounted a ground of rejoicing.

Yet once more, and to sum up what we have said in one word, this faith embraces God as a Father. Who can tell the significance of this name, or measure the extent of its consolation? The Father—such was the title which Jesus delighted to give to the Supreme Being, the Creator, Preserver, and Governor; in which he comprised all the ideas that these terms represent, and by which he taught us to address the God of nature, of providence, and of grace. The Father, whose regard for us, whose constant, watchful, tender love no other word would denote, who chose, by referring to the inexpressible yearnings, the unconquerable affection, of the parental bosom, to signify his own disposition towards us—the Father is the object of Christian faith, of that faith which is but another name for filial sentiment, for childlike trust, for heartfelt piety. "Let not your heart be troubled!" And why not? "Ye believe in God," whom I have revealed as the Father. Could Jesus have given a stronger reason?

He added however—"believe," or "ye believe also in me." What is the faith in Christ that can compose our griefs and subdue our anxieties? It is faith in him as the beloved and chosen of the Father, in whom we behold the messenger, representative, and image of the ever-blessed God. It is faith in him as the kindest of friends, who brought from heaven inestimable gifts, and sacrificed his life to insure their transmission to future ages. It is faith in him as the authority for those truths which have just now been reviewed, by which the soul is made to feel the presence and love of the Infinite One. It is faith in him as the pattern, whose character we should adopt for our standard of judgment and our goal of effort, from whose life we should learn how to do good, from whose death how to suffer evil. It is faith in him as one who has "brought life and immortality to light," who has taken away the vain terrors of death and shown us the home to which death is but the passage. It is faith in that divine influence of which he is the type, and in that glorious consummation of which he is the pledge,—the influence which sanctifies the humble, and the consummation which will present them redeemed from sin and infirmity, and all that oppressed and all that afflicted them here, an innumerable company, partakers of the heaven in the dawning of whose light they had walked on earth. "Let not your heart be troubled." And why not? "Ye believe in me," whose word is truth, whose spirit is love, whose gift is peace, whose promise is eternal life. What more could he have said?

The effects of such a faith are obvious. It takes away fear, banishes distrust, excludes or moderates anxiety, and sheds an influence over the soul like that which music exerts on susceptible natures, overpowering their passions and soothing their griefs to rest. But it produces no dreamy indolence. It quickens into generous action the faculties which it releases from the bondage of impatient desire, and invigorates the soul which it tranquillizes, fulfilling the promise, "in quietness and in confidence shall be your strength." There is stillness, but not the silence of sleep; repose, but not the torpor of apathy. There is effort, struggle, conflict, self-denial; but over the whole internal world reigns the spirit of order, and this spirit is sustained in the exercise of its authority by the faith which persuades every sentiment and desire into obedience. There is a spiritual energy which is mightier than any violence of passion, yet is manifested only in the calmness which it diffuses throughout the character and over the whole life, a calmness which no one mistakes for unnatural or artificial composure, but all, even the most selfish, behold with admiration, and all, even the most careless and vicious, wish they might possess when their triai comes. The soul is indeed deeply moved, but it looks to God, and in the Father's face sees the justification of its confidence through every change. "If it be possible, let this cup pass from me," may be its silent prayer, when it perceives the impending calamity, yet before the blow has fallen it adds—"not my will, but thine be done." Come what may, it cannot even suspect that there should be forgetfulness or error; and therefore it surrenders itself to the disposal of a love which is never swayed by blind, impulses, nor ever betrayed into unwise measures. The Being who afflicts is the Being in whom it trusts. In its trouble it goes to Him from whom trouble comes, for he is "the God of all comfort," and with him dwell peace and hope. The divine presence is, in the fine language of the prophet, "like a serene heat when the sun shineth, like a dewy cloud in the heat of harvest." Hence there are no repinings, no secret complaints, no half-sceptical surmisings, no anxious forebodings, no rebellion of spirit, no reluctance of will. But when most afflicted, the Christian is not disquieted in vain, since he has remembered the counsel of the Psalmist, "Hope thou in God;" or if in his extremity he should be compelled to cry out, as did the ancient servant of God, "I am feeble and sore-broken, I have roared by reason of the disquietness of my heart," yet he can add, "Lord, all my desire is before thee, and my groaning is not hid from thee. In thee, O Lord, do I hope." Such is the effect of true religious faith in time of trouble.

It is still a question of interest, how faith obtains this efficacy. A few words will contain the answer. It is in the first place a reasonable faith, the understanding admitting the justice of that control which it exerts ove the heart. Can any thing be more reasonable than that we should believe in God, or that believing we should trust in him? Is not the universe full of the evidences of his being, is it not inscribed all over with the marks of his perfections, must not he do his pleasure here and everywhere, and ought not we to rejoice in his supreme dominion? "Shall not the Judge of all the earth do right?" was the inquiry of one, who ages before the birth of the Savior thus expressed his confidence in the Divine rectitude. Shall not our Father do what is best? is the still stronger appea which the heart may make when beset by manifold trials, now that Jesus has made known the paternal love of the Supreme. Wil' any one of us, ignorant as we are, arraign his dealings, and refuse to adore his will, because we cannot see its issues: when the very affliction that confronts us may be the most fruitfu blessing that he could send? Perfect trust in God is altogether reasonable. And not less reasonable is it to believe in Christ, who gav such clear and abundant proofs of his mission Reliance on him is as just as it is consolatory.

Have the truths which beam from his cross so little divinity, or do they import so little, that he is a weak man who draws comfort from them? No, no. Reason refuses its assent.

But not only is the understanding convinced, the affections are addressed. They are not left bleeding and helpless when stricken down by the providence of God. The busy and the happy may pass them by, like the priest and the Levite of the parable; but Christian faith, like the good Samaritan, approaches them and comforts them with its gentle offices of sympathy, and lifts them up and bears them in its arms to the Father's presence. There they find a place of repose, where their wounds are healed, and they recover strength, while learning those exercises which can never involve disappointment. The pure love of earth becomes the everlasting love of heaven.

The hopes too experience the protection of faith. It raises them from the dust, and replumes their shattered wings, that they may soar on high and pursue their course through regions of immortality. How can the Christian be troubled who in the future sees infinite progress, unbroken union, and perpetual happiness? How can he be troubled, whose hopes have already penetrated the mansions which Jesus went from earth to prepare, and have conversed there with the honored and loved whom this world has lost?

Yet once more; this faith is pre-eminently practical, calling the soul to duty and bestowing upon it the ability to persevere. It forbids idle regrets and profitless contemplations, and while it violates not the sanctity of the past, it summons the energies to do the work of the present, whatever it be. It rebukes that habit of grief which feeds itself with bitter thoughts, as alike unjust to God and injurious to the soul. It makes obedience at once the test and security of solace, and by interesting both the mind and the heart in the duties which are waiting for performance, it lightens the burthen of sorrow and provides the satisfactions of virtuous effort.

With such connections and influences, can any person wonder at the effects of faith? The extent of its efficiency may be still farther illustrated by considering the subjects and the occasions that prove its power. It may be cherished by every one, and none by whom it is cherished will fail to receive its consolation. There is not a man on earth too high to be controlled by its authority, nor too low to be reached by its pity. It addresses to the learned truths which human study never could evolve from the mysteries of the universe. It bestows on the rich support which all their wealth could not buy. It offers its counsel to the young, and its solace to the aged. Infirmity leans upon the staff which this heavenly visitant puts into its hand, while ignorance rejoices to be made wise in the knowledge which it communicates, and poverty seizes on the revelations which are better than all earthly treasures. It is human nature which cries out for its assistance, and since the elements of this nature are in all men the same, faith must be a benefactor to all. Amidst the Alpine recesses of Switzerland, and in the lowly hut of the Greenlander, there have been prayers and rejoicings and consolations and hopes at the very moment when they were heard in the cathedrals of England, and felt in the hearts of titled men and noble women who feared God and loved the Savior amidst all the splendor of their high estate. Want is universal, and fear is universal, and love is universal, but faith is mightier than they all, and can comfort every soul which they afflict.

And again, there is no condition so disastrous, no calamity so severe, no suffering so extreme, that let it fall upon rich or poor, high or low, wise or simple, old or young, Christian faith cannot furnish the relief and solace which are needed. No occasion can arise which shall set its power at defiance. Of this the history of Jesus affords the strongest possible illustration. He was sustained by his faith in the hours of his temptation and his affliction. It was in reference to his own sudden and fearful death, which he anticipated, not by a vague presentiment such as sometimes gives warning to the heart of its near separation from the scenes of earth, but by prophetic foreknowledge—it was under the clear vision of Gethsemane and Pilate's judgment-hall and Calvary, that he held that most touching conversation with his disciples, in which he aimed to infuse into their minds his own serenity. And as the events of that awful day when crucifixion sealed a life of innocence and closed a heaven-appointed ministry drew near, and he could not repress the exclamation, "My soul is exceeding sorrowful," he recovered himself from the dejection into which he was sinking by a triumphant exercise of faith in his Father, the same who is our Father and our God. If we turn from the Savior to his apostles, their situation gives new force to his words. What a disappointment was hanging over them—how deep a darkness it was that would soon envelop them—how heavy a sorrow that would fall on their hearts! Their Master, their friend, their stay taken from them by a violent death, and they left to struggle alone with the evils of life a thousand fold aggravated by their late indulgence of delightful expectations. Yet with reference to this calamity Jesus said to them, "Let not your heart be troubled: ye believe in God, ye believe also in me;" as if he would teach them that no change could come so unexpected or so extensive or so heart-rending, that their faith might not be a sufficient solace.

These are examples for our instruction. They show us that in the gloomiest hours we may be supported and comforted by our faith. Let it be that the heaviest stroke which the Divine providence could inflict has fallen upon our hearts, it must not, for it need not, crush them. They may still be firm and tranquil. Let it be that the pleasant home is made desolate, and the affections which had been justly awakened are denied further indulgence, and the hopes on which Heaven seemed to smile have become like bitter dust, and the society in which we were rejoicing is exchanged for loneliness, and the sympathies which we were strengthening can be nourished only in imagination, and the duties which we were looking to another to help us in performing must be discharged by our single fidelity, and the life which seemed to promise a harvest of ever-growing and ever-ripening satisfactions appears now like a waste over which a burning wind has swept, and let it be that all this reverse has come upon us in a moment, and all this suffering struck home at a single blow; still "let not our heart be troubled." Let it cleave to God and to the Savior. Let it look up, to the Father's benignant countenance, never more benignant than when seen through the clouds of affliction; let it look forward, to the immortality where patience shall have its recompense, and trust shall realize its hope, and love shall be more precious for its earthly trials, and sadness shall never mingle in the soul's experience; let it look inward, to the spiritual nature of which it is a part, and which is developed and perfected by discipline; let it look abroad, and see duties in which it can find healthful and useful employment. Let it believe in God, let it believe in Christ—let it have a true faith, and it will not be troubled. It will be clothed with resignation, it will be armed with fortitude. It will remember past mercies, and be grateful; it will consider present engagements, and be ready to feel and to pray for others; it will commit its destiny to the Lord, and doing his will receive with meekness the chastisements, while it lays hold on the promises, of his love.

In these remarks we have but glanced at some of the topics of Christian faith, particularly at that great doctrine of immortality, to which the heart turns with special interest in the time of affliction. The value of this doctrine, and of others on which something has been said, it is the object of the following pages to exhibit.

They contain selections from English and American writers, whose names are familiar in this community,—Price, Cappe, Channing, Dewey, Palfrey, Parker, Colman and others. Many of the pieces here printed will be recognised as of recent publication. The idea of preparing the present volume arose out of the belief that these materials if brought together would constitute a valuable book of consolation. Other extracts of a similar character have been added; and upon whatever page the reader may open, it is believed that he will find "words of comfort." That they may soothe the grief of bereavement, and lighten the load of trouble under which the heart even of the Christian is often ready to faint, is the hope and prayer of the compiler.

E. S. G.

Boston, March, 1836.

THE GOOD OF AFFLICTION.

"It is good for me that I have been afflicted:"—happy would it be for us if this were our sentiment, and if our hearts thus reposed in Providence. How tranquil would our soul be, if, persuaded that God, while he has disposed all events for the greatest good of his creatures, retains them under his ceaseless control, we were able to confide in him in all the circumstances of our life, and to see in the dispensations which appear at first the most inauspicious, the advantages which will subsequently result. Unhappily, these are not our thoughts, this is not our language. Not that our doubt extends to the dealings of Providence in general: we are not blind enough for that. We believe that God conducts the whole of the world, that he has regulated and arranged every thing with the deepest wisdom; and we place the most entire confidence in him as long as our lot is happy: but does it change, are our plans traversed, are we visited by affliction, and exposed to the storms of life,—then our confidence in Providence wavers; we see no longer that wisdom and that goodness which we used to admire in his ways; we can no longer harmonize with his tenderness the evils he permits us to experience; God appears to have abandoned us, and murmurs are ready to escape from our lips. "How unhappy I am: my fortune has received a check, from which it will never recover!" "He is gone, my husband, the sole support of my children, and I am undone!" "That calumny has dishonored me forever; the idea of it will be the torment of my life!" Foolish complaints, unjustifiable distrust! God is ever a tender Father to us, even when he exposes us to the blows of adversity; and those afflictions, through which he leads us, may prove to us of incalculable advantage. This is what I now propose to show.

We are exposed consequently to sufferings. Many of us perhaps groan now under the weight of some calamity. Those who are in prosperity may be on the point of falling. Evil, ever present or at hand, threatens us all. Come, then, all of us, and let us arm ourselves against its blows, and draw consoling thoughts from religion: come, and learn from it to what an extent the very evils of which we complain may, if we knew how to profit by them, produce the happiest consequences.

When we are well convinced that God has each of us constantly under his notice; that he wishes the happiness of us all, and that he has in his power a thousand means to lead us to it, we are naturally induced to ask why, this being the case, he often leaves us in, yea exposes us to, misfortune; and we can find no other reason, except that our afflictions have their uses, seen of God, but unknown to us, and that what we call evil is really good. This conclusion is confirmed by the Holy Scriptures in many places. They often represent the different troubles of life as benefits from God; they tell us that he chastens those whom he loves, and that our transient sufferings produce an infinite weight of glory. What, then, is that happiness which we buy so dearly, that, to lead us to acquire it, He who is our Father exposes us sometimes to many and long calamities? He tells us himself. It is through much tribulation that we may be fitted for entering on the happiness of heaven; that we may be rendered partakers of his holiness. "It is good," said David, after having learnt by experience, "it is good for me to have been afflicted, that I may learn thy statutes: before I went astray, but now I keep thy word." It is, then, to perfect our characters, to render us worthy of the happiness which God has in reserve for the righteous, that he subjects us to the reverses of which we complain; that he deprives one of his fortune; that he takes from another a beloved child; that he allows the reputation of a third to be torn by calumny. Doubtless, if God took counsel of flesh and blood, he would pursue a different course. Doubtless, if he left to our will the removal of evils, at the moment when they are on the point of falling on our heads, most, perhaps all of us, would sacrifice to the ease and gratification of life the inestimable advantages which may accrue to us from momentary calamities. There are undoubtedly persons who are in a state to compare the afflictions of this world with the fruits they produce in the next, and who can judge which is preferable here, a portion of evil, or constant prosperity. But God, who judges better still; God, who weighs in the balance some years of bitterness against an eternity of bliss; God, who loves us and has disposed every thing for our greatest good, places us sometimes in the school of misfortune, in consideration of the great advantages which may result;—for adversity makes us enter into our own breasts, and reminds us of our sins; it humbles our pride; it detaches us from the world; whilst prosperity produces the opposite effects.

Adversity, I remarked, makes us enter into our own hearts, and reminds us of our sins. The afflictions to which God exposes us, I know, are not always a natural consequence of our faults; at least, it is not easy to discover this connection in every instance, and sometimes they fall on men in whose conduct there is nothing criminal. But, in the most virtuous there are many failures, and often serious faults. Whilst prosperity continues, they are not seen. Imagination lends to every object a smiling aspect, and men see even themselves in the same pleasing light. A certain undefinable intoxication is inseparable from success. This blinds even the good; conceals their faults from their own sight, and sometimes transforms them into virtues. Alas! who of us does not know this fatal intoxication,—who of us, when the present is smiling, when hope is embellishing the future, when joy circulates throughout his frame, has not felt a certain esteem for himself, which prevented him from sounding his heart; an indulgence which excused all faults, and extolled the least excellencies? Whilst the children of Jacob lived around their father in the bosom of tranquillity and opulence, they thought not of the cruelty which they had been guilty of in selling their brother Joseph into slavery; but they remembered their crime when in Egypt, and when menaced with prison and death. Thirty years after their atrocious sin, remorse awakens in their hardened hearts. "We," they say, "are verily guilty concerning our brother, in that we saw the anguish of his soul and would not hear; therefore is this distress come upon us." O Adversity! thou art the true friend of man! thou dost not blind him; thou dost not mislead him by perfidious flatteries; thou makest him enter into his own bosom; thou presentest to him the mirror of truth; thou showest him, what without thee he would never have seen, his own heart, with its weaknesses, its sins, its vicious inclinations. What a sight! At first he is humbled, saddened, confounded; but from this mental confusion soon there ensue repentance, energy, christian resolutions, and on this rich foundation divine grace raises the edifice of his salvation!

But afflictions have another and most valuable advantage, that of humbling our pride. This vice, which is so contrary to our nature, from which our weakness, our imperfections, our dependence on all around us, ought for so many reasons to keep us free; this vice, which is the source of many others, which almost always engenders impiety and licentiousness, which is itself rebellion against God, and, as he himself has declared, one of the most offensive in his sight; this vice, which certainly excludes him who is guilty of it from eternal happiness—pride, we know, insinuates itself, and springs up too easily in our hearts. Whilst we live in moderate circumstances, it does not commonly make great progress; but in the rays of prosperity it grows, extends, produces fruit. At first we are disposed to ascribe our success to Providence; but in proportion as it increases—in proportion, that is, as Providence blesses our efforts, we lose sight of its agency: to ourselves, to our labors we attribute our prosperity; it is our own industry that increases our riches, and secures the wisdom of our enterprises; it is our own merit that draws on us public consideration, and advances us in the world; it is the goodness of our character that gives us friends. The admiration we feel towards ourselves is, we soon fancy, felt by others. We raise ourselves above them; we affect distinguished manners; we forget those with whom we had been previously connected; we display before their sight a luxury that astonishes them; we become harsh, imperious to our inferiors, lofty and exacting with our equals; without compassion towards the unfortunate. Soon does he, whom fortune has always favored, persuade himself that it has no longer the power to abandon him; that he is himself the arbiter of his lot: he no longer thinks that his life, his talents, his happiness, his all comes to him from God; that on him he depends for every thing. In this infatuation, swollen with pride, he casts around him his disdainful eyes, and exclaims, "I am alone; there is none but me on the earth;" and, in the spirit of Nebuchadnezzar, "Is not this the great Babylon, which I have built by my power, for my royal abode?" and, in the spirit of Alexander, dazzled with his success, forgets that he is a man; forgets even God himself.

What can recall him from this intoxication? Nothing but the blows of adversity can work this miracle. God thunders from the highest heavens, "Cut down the tree; scatter its fruit; disperse its foliage." Against this man; "Let him be deprived of those riches which have inflated his heart;"—against another, "Let calumny blacken his reputation, he has been greedy of honor;"—against a third, "Let him be cast in disgrace from that dignity to which his ambition had caused him to ascend." O God of judgment! how terrible, yet how salutary are thy inflictions! They scatter, as by enchantment, those mists of vanity with which the proud man had been bewildered; they destroy that scaffolding of ambitious projects that he had constructed. Then he renounces those vain grandeurs which were the aliment of his pride and arrogance; he learns to be modest towards his fellow-creatures, compassionate to the unfortunate. He sees himself as he is, poor, wretched, and naked; he acknowledges that all his talents, his qualities, his advantages, all that he has, come from God, and he humbles himself under his powerful hand. It is thus that the blows of Providence, which take from us the objects of our affections, destroy our pride.

They do still more; they detach our hearts from earth, and direct them to heaven. What a multitude of good things have been shed on our abode! How is every thing arranged for the happiness of the beings who dwell here! Objects which flatter our senses; beauties which gladden our imaginations; above all, sentiments which transport our souls —the sublime exertions of generosity, of virtue—the sweet affections of friendship, of humanity, of patriotism—all unite to render us happy, and attach us to this world. Yet it is not our country; it is only a place of passage, only a vestibule to lead us to our true dwelling. For what is it destined? Not to engross our affections; but to instruct us, to prepare our souls for enjoyments of a nobler order, to render them fit for a purer happiness. If, however, it is so magnificent, what must be the beauties of the home to which we tend; what must be the joys which are in reserve for us; what must be the transports which are prepared for our hearts in that place of perfection where God himself dwells? But we think not of it, we forget it; yes, that world of felicity, the road to which Jesus has marked and trod, which God offers as the recompense of virtue, and the conquest of which ought to be the great end of our life, excites but feebly our desires, and kindles but slightly our ambition. The flowers that we meet in the road of life cause us to lose sight of this grand object: dazzled by brilliant trifles, we retard our progress towards solid good; we say with Peter, "It is good for us to be here; let us make ourselves tents;" we grow attached to earth; the idea of leaving it fills us with alarm. Fools that we are! such is our love for this world, that we should be satisfied never to leave it; that we should consent to exchange what is every thing for what is nothing; that ocean of felicity for a few pleasures of little value!

But God, who sees our blindness, pities us; mingles bitterness with the sweets of this life; takes from us the coveted good, when we are on the point of seizing it—the objects of our affections, in the moment when we think our possession sure. This man had placed his heart on riches; God snatches them away: another, on a beloved child; God smites it in its father's embrace. One lived only for friendship—lived by the attachment of those to whom he was ever doing good; and God allows his reward to be treachery and ingratitude. Another longed for glory; instead he gives him disgrace. Under these blows the soul is broken down; for a time it is unable to recover from its griefs; it feels an immense void; a deep melancholy consumes it; on every side it searches for consolation; finding none, it turns upon itself. What terrible blows have struck my heart! the Christian exclaims: how gloomy this world appears! What folly to fix my heart upon it! It is filled only with unreal objects. I stretch out my hand to seize riches, they fly away; I open my arms to embrace my child, he is gone; I have exhausted the cup of life, there remains but bitter dregs. All my property, all my friends, all that I loved, abandons me. O, my God and Father! the reason is, thou wishest to draw me to thyself: thou snatchest away perishable good, because thou wishest to secure for me permanent good; thou disappointest my affections, that I may direct them on him who will never deceive; thou takest its brightness from the splendor of the world; thou renderest its pleasures tasteless; thou causest me to find pain in what constituted my happiness. Ah! the reason is, thou wishest to turn my view toward those happy shores; to seek, to covet, to lay hold on that life, in which are found real joys, supreme beauty, true riches; thou callest me from the heavens; thou encouragest me to take my flight to those happy mansions, to follow those whom my heart loves. I hear thy voice, tender Father; I yield to thy invitations;

I desire to depart hence and be with Christ.

Thus, then, those afflictions which we dreaded, and of which we complained, may produce the most happy consequences. Yes, "it is good for us to be afflicted." If we lived always in prosperity, we should never enter into our own breasts, and should therefore remain ignorant of our sins; inordinate pride would inflate our hearts; we should be so attached to the earth and its miserable pleasures, as to desire never to quit them. But adversity awakens our soul by its salutary shocks; it dissipates that charm which embellishes, in our eyes, the deformity of our conduct; it prostrates our pride, and detaches us from the false good of this world, to make us aspire to that which is unalloyed with pain, and which will be unlimited in duration. The remedy is bitter, the operation is painful, but it is necessary for our salvation. "Chastisement," says Paul, "is for the present not joyous, but grievous; nevertheless, it yieldeth the peaceable fruit of righteousness to them who are exercised thereby." A child weeps, rebels, because his father subjects him to a severe discipline, and makes him undergo the toil of study: he does not foresee the advantages which will subsequently accrue to him. We, in the same way, dread afflictions, weep, rebel, despair, when God makes them our portion. Why? We do not know all the good that they are fitted to communicate; we do not know how many evils they cause us to avoid, how much happiness they will produce. But a day is coming when we shall know it, when we shall congratulate ourselves on our exposure to sorrow, when we shall bless our Heavenly Father for the way in which he led us to himself. As a traveller, arrived at his beloved home, feels a pleasure in retracing in his mind and recounting in his family the woes he has felt, the dangers he has run, the mischances he has experienced, so we, arrived in our heavenly country, shall contemplate with ravishment all the pains we underwent on the journey of life; shall dwell with satisfaction on the crosses we have found; be filled with surprise in discovering the wise designs of Providence in our afflictions, and the numberless benefits which have resulted from them. We, who know and feel the truth of these assertions, will never tire in blessing our Father, in adoring him for all he has done for us; especially for those trials which, in spite of our tears, our cries, our murmurs, he has caused us to experience.

O tender Father, who ceasest not to be occupied with our happiness, and who, by ways to us unknown, conductest us to a felicity far above all our thoughts; pardon the doubts, the complaints, that we sometimes allow to escape from our lips against thy wise and benignant dispensations. Thou knowest we are feeble and ignorant. Our ways are not thy ways, we acknowledge at this holy hour. And forever do we abjure our murmurs, lay aside our distrust, place ourselves under thy guidance. Whatever thou decidest, we will submit, adore, and have no other care but to please thee, by observing thy holy will.

THE MOURNER COMFORTED.

"Blessed are they that mourn, for they shall find
Comfort and joy!" Though flesh and blood rebel
'Gainst heaven-ward thoughts, and the vext spirit swell
With anxious tossings, still, the veil behind
Of earth-born mists, the faith-directed mind
Sees throned in cloudless light the INVISIBLE,
At whose right hand delights in fullness dwell,
And bliss forever lasting. Be resigned,
Thou child of sorrow, to his sovereign will;
Drink, as he bids, the bitter cup, and bear
Thy cross in patience! From the holy hill
A gleam shall cheer thee, till, safe-harbored there
Thou feel how faintly earth's severest ill
May with the weight of heavenly joys compare.

ERRONEOUS VIEWS OF DEATH.

CHRISTIANITY was designed to introduce into the world new views and feelings concerning death. We seem to see its character and office typified in the visit of Jesus to the house of Mary and Martha, on occasion of the death of their brother. It was a house of affliction. Wailing and lamentation were heard in it, as they are, at one time or another, in all the dwellings of this world. But our blessed Savior approached it in a calm consciousness that he was commissioned with a doctrine and clothed with a power that would triumph over death; that death, in fact, was not the end nor the interruption of existence; that death indeed was only death in appearance, while in reality the spirit's life is progressive, ever continued, immortal. What less do his words import than the annunciation to the world of this new view of mortality? "I am the resurrection and the life: he that believeth in me, though he were dead, yet shall he live: and whosoever liveth and believeth in me, shall *never* die"—shall die not, at all, forever! The apostles, in like manner, evidently considered themselves as commissioned to teach new views of death. They taught the Christian converts to "sorrow not as others who had no hope." They represented the coming of Christ as designed to "deliver those who through fear of death were all their lifetime subject to bondage."

Christianity, we repeat, was designed to introduce into the world new views of death and futurity. But in this, as in several other respects, we apprehend that it has made as yet but a feeble impression upon the mass of those who have received it. They have not yet partaken of the cheerfulness, tranquillity, and triumph of him who "has abolished death, and brought life and immortality to light in the gospel." They have not so "lived and believed" in Jesus as triumphantly to feel that they "shall never die!" There is more, we are tempted to say, of heathen despondency and dread among us, than of christian hope and trust.

We shall speak of this subject not without solemnity and the tenderness due to a theme so affecting—of these we can scarcely fail—but we shall not speak of it with an awe that forbids us to reason upon it. We shall speak of death as those who, God helping, do not fear it with any excessive and unreasonable dread. We believe that it is the great course of nature, the appointment of God, a wise and good appointment, and that it is to be met with pious submission, calmness, and trust. We believe in One, who has destroyed "the power of death;" who has come to deliver us from this very fear that has struck so deep a horror into the world, who has unfolded to us the bright and exalting hope of an endless and blessed life.

The dread which is felt of this event has manifested itself in many popular impressions of the most erroneous and indefensible, as well as painful, character.

There prevails an erroneous or an exaggerated idea of many of the circumstances that attend the dying hour.

In particular, it is thought that this final event passes with some dreadful visitation of unknown agony over the departing sufferer. It is imagined that there is some strange and mysterious reluctance in the spirit to leave the body; that it struggles long to retain its hold, and is at last torn with violence from its mortal tenement; and in fine, that this conflict between the soul and the body greatly adds to the pangs of dissolution. But it may be justly presumed, from what usually appears, that there is no particular nor acute suffering; not more than is often experienced in life; nay, rather, that there is less, because the very powers of suffering are enfeebled, the very capacities of pain are nearly exhausted. Death is to be regarded rather as a sleep than an acute sensation, as a suspension rather than a conflict of our faculties. Our Savior once said in relation to this event, "Our friend Lazarus sleepeth." The martyr Stephen, we are told, "fell asleep," though he died amidst the blows and shouts of murderers. And the Scripture denominates the pious dead, "those who sleep in Jesus." Death is the sleep of the weary. It is repose, the body's repose, after the busy and toilsome day of life.

We have all witnessed perhaps the progress of this change; and what was it? Let our senses and our understanding answer; and not our imagination. What was it, but gradually diminishing strength, feeble utterance, failing perception, and total insensibility? The change, as it passed before us, may have been attended with accidental circumstances of mental experience or bodily sensation; but the change itself, death considered as an event, was only a gradual decline and extinction of the powers of life. This is all which we saw, or could know, as necessarily belonging to this crisis in the progress of our being. And yet, from this ignorance, we allow ourselves to be troubled by the phantoms of agitating conjecture. We imagine, and indeed it is common to say, that because "no one has returned to tell us what it is to die," there must be some mysterious and peculiar sensation, some awful physical experience attending it. But we see nothing, we see indications of nothing, and we ought not to presume any thing of this nature.

Neither are we to presume that death arouses the mind, in the last moments of its earthly existence, to the keenest attention, or to the most intense action of its powers. The subject, when distinctly contemplated beforehand, may do so; it may often do so in the midst of life; and well were it, if it far more frequently aroused us to do in season the work of life. All we wish to say is,—and we wish to say it to preclude all appeals at once to mysterious fear and unfounded hope—that there is no peculiar, no fearful nor hopeful activity of mind amidst the solemnities of dissolution; that, in most cases, there is no activity. It is probable, that the exhausted faculties usually sink to their mortal repose, as they do to nightly sleep; and that the convulsive struggles which are sometimes witnessed, are often as unconscious as those with which we sink to the slumbers of evening rest.

Nor, when the veil of delirium is spread over the mortal hour, can we regard it as the evil that it is often thought to be. It has seemed to us rather, in many cases, as a friendly veil, drawn by the hand of nature over what would otherwise be the agonies of separation, over the anguish that the parent would feel at leaving children orphans and destitute, or that the friend would feel in saying farewell to those who were dearest upon earth. Delirium often interposes, we believe, by the kind providence of God, where nature would be too weak, or faith too infirm for the trial.

Nor yet is there any thing but fancy in what is sometimes said of the loneliness of the last hour. To the selfish and the bad, and in proportion as they possess this character, there is indeed solitude in death, and it may then be doubly felt. But to them there is solitude also in life; solitude in the chamber of sickness, in the hour of retired meditation, nay, and it is oftentimes deeply felt in the throng of society. If we deserve to have friends, they are with us in death as truly as in life; so long as we are conscious of any thing earthly, we are conscious of their presence. It may sustain and soothe us, till the last moment of our stay on earth. "I walked with her,"—said one who laid down the remains of a beloved companion in a distant land—"I walked with her down the valley of shadows; I wiped the cold damps of death from her forehead; and saw her ascend to the mansions of the blessed!"

But we must hasten briefly to consider some of the errors that relate, not to the circumstances, but to the nature, the essential character of this solemn event.

When our Savior says, "He that liveth and believeth in me shall never die," he adds, "believest thou this?" The question might still be put to multitudes even in a Christian land, and, we doubt not, with the strongest implication of their unbelief. They do not believe it. Death is regarded as the extinction, rather than as the continuance of being. Whatever the words of our theology may say, the real impression upon most minds is, that death sunders almost all the ties that united us to our former existence; that it changes not only our state, but our nature; that the soul, as it travels to the "undiscovered country," is passing beyond the borders of all that it has known, and sought, and valued. We are apt to feel as if on the passage from life we parted with all that our thoughts had familiarized and our affections cherished. But is not this an error? We take with us—so to speak—our thinking and conscious selves; and it is no vanity, but a simple truth, to say, in a very important sense, that ourself is our all; for it embraces all our mental acquisitions and attachments, our joys and hopes, our attainments of piety, our treasures of knowledge, all elevated and holy contemplations that we may have indulged in, all our habits of thought and feeling that are estimable and pure, all that is precious in happiness, all that is sacred in memory; and the record of all this death will not erase, but will only impress upon it the seal of perpetuity. It has not erased these things, we may believe, from the venerated and pious minds that have gone before us. The dead,—the departed, should we rather say,—are connected with us by more than the ties of memory. The love that on earth yearned towards us is not dead; the kindness that gladdened us is not dead; the sympathy that bound itself with our fortunes is not dead, nor has it lost its fervor, surely, in the pity of an angel. No; if our Christian guides speak truly, it still yearns towards us, it would still gladden us. It still melts in tenderness over our sorrows. The world of spirits—we know not where it is, whether far or near; but it may as well, for all that we can understand, be near to us, as far distant; and in that fervent love, which knows nothing of change or distance or distinction, it is forever near us. Our friend, if he be the same and not another being—our friend, in whatever world, in whatever sphere, is still our friend. The ties of every virtuous union are, like the virtue which cements them, like the affections of angels, like the love of God which binds them to the eternal throne, immortal.

The evil of making this wide separation, this violent disruption of the present from the future, as well as of other prevailing views of death, is in many ways great. Our thoughts do not easily pass to live in the future, or to draw from it the motives of action. Our theological views of this subject, our contemplations of futurity, are too much like the ancient poetic dreams of an Elysian land and a Tartarean region, visionary and ineffectual. There is a fearful retribution, there is a sublime beatitude, we admit; but our conceptions of both are vague and unreal; and our fear does not deter us from sin, and our hope does not allure us to purity and heaven. Between us and our future recompense we look upon death as "a great gulf fixed," and it cuts off the communication of our thoughts. Between the good and the bad a great gulf is fixed indeed, but not between us and the departed. Death is not that gulf; yet we so regard it. We do not sufficiently consider it as a stage, a necessary stage in the progress of being; as a natural passage from the childhood to the maturity of our existence. We are deterred too from the thoughts of futurity by the imaginary glooms and mysteries of the entrance to it. Even the most attractive ideas of a future life, even a spiritual relish for its joys, and a conscience free from alarms, could scarcely overcome our reluctance to so fearful and dismal an approach to it. We could hardly think of home, or welcome the prospect of admission there, if we must pass to it through unknown conflicts and woes, if we could reach it only by braving the horrors of shipwreck, if we could gain its threshold only by rushing over the burning ruins of a conflagration.

Again; death is commonly regarded as the visitation of God's wrath, as the fruit and punishment of sin. We do not forget the language of Scripture on this subject; that "death entered into the world by sin, and so death passed upon all men, for that all have sinned." It is to be remembered, however, that in many passages where death is said to be the fruit of sin the word death is used figuratively; that mortality is not meant, but misery. This may be seen in the whole of that account which is given of Paul's experience and reasonings in the seventh and eighth chapters of the Epistle to the Romans; and in other instances. And upon the text before quoted it has been justly argued, that the death which "entered by sin" is not the specific calamity of being mortal, but all the evil brought upon us by sin, including whatever is evil in mortality itself. That all this is meant by the word death, we say, has been argued from the circumstance, that it is set in contrast with all the benefits derived from the interposition of our Savior. As these benefits include more than mere continuance of life, so, it is contended, the contrasted evil which sin is said to introduce cannot be death to the body merely, but rather death to the soul; that is, misery, fear, disquietude and gloom. And it might be still more strongly urged, with reference to this point, that, if mortality were the specific and only evil meant in that passage, it is said to be removed by the interposition of our Savior. This is the very point which we are laboring to establish. Jesus Christ "has abolished death, and brought life and immortality to light in the gospel." He has presented new views of mortality. He has taught us, that it is the death of the body only; that the good man, that the spirit of goodness which is in him, that the intrinsic and intellectual being, "shall never die."

We are not however anxious to deny, for it is obviously true, that sin has given a complexion to this event; that it has, to a certain extent, connected pain, and doubt, and gloom with mortality. In some respects we can see this influence. Sin, which partly consists in the undue indulgence of the body, has made all our diseases more severe and painful. Sin too has clouded and darkened the mind, and filled it with inquietude and fear. Sin then, we repeat, has given a complexion to this event. It has made our departure from this world. not a translation, but a death.

Yet surely the departure, simply considered, is not to be regarded as an ordination of God's wrath, but of his infinite goodness. Whatever is universal and unavoidable must always be held to be good. Sin only, the choice of man, is essentially evil. Events, laws, the ordinances of God, are ever good. When we approach the dwelling where death has entered, when we join the circle of mourning friends and kindred over which the mortal stroke has just brought its stupefying horror or its heart-rending agony, when that solemn silence, that dread vacuity of death is around us, broken only by the sighs and shudderings of grief and despair, we are apt at first to feel as if we stood in some awful chasm where God is not, or in some overshadowing cloud where he is present only in displeasure. But when we remember that this is the inevitable lot, that there are thousands of such scenes passing every hour on earth, ten thousand human hearts rent with like sorrow, we are ready to ask—Can this universal fate be otherwise than an ordination of wisdom and goodness? Can the unvarying allotment, to which all the children of God are subject, be vindictive? Can that which befalls all earthly beings, fills all time, and spreads before the eye of Heaven such an uninterrupted scene—can it be a signal measure of God's wrath? The catastrophe, in the darkest view of it, would not be so horrible as the supposition which thus explains it.

Besides, a dissolution of the body, and a departure from this world, result from the very nature and necessity of things. The human frame is not made to live always, and the earth as evidently was not designed to support the accumulating generations of mankind. Nay, more; departure at some time or other from this life, so far from being a penal requisition, must to every reflecting mind appear in the highest degree desirable. Let the question be put to our calmer and loftier reflections, and there can be no other answer. *Would* we live always? Would we always bear the burden of imperfection and infirmity? Would we always pant for knowledge and happiness that we cannot attain; and shall we ever cling to that load of flesh, and of all the ills that flesh is heir to, which drags us down to the earth? No; we would die; we would depart; we would be released and be at rest. We might desire to mount on the winged chariot of Elijah; but it has pleased God to appoint for us a different way. Be it so, that it is for our sins, or that our sins have cast a shadow over the passage out of this world; shall we not then the more humbly and submissively yield ourselves to it?—not with terror, not with slavish dread, for God does not chasten, even for our sins, in unpitying wrath, but in tender mercy.

We would not then live always. Earth could not bear us. Humanity could not bear its load. Still more; the mind could not be satisfied. It would ask for other scenes, for other regions, for other sources of knowledge, for other fountains of joy.

We would depart, then; and this is but saying that we would die. We must yield our powers to the sleep of death, that we may awake to a new life. We must change the form and mode of our existence, that we may exist in a higher sphere. We must cease to live as men, that we may begin to live as angels. The unsightly worm must sink to inaction and death, that it may rise from its grovelling in the dust, that it may become an inhabitant of the air, that it may unfold its wings in a new region, and become the creature of life and beauty that God designed it to be. The soul in like manner must drop its "mortal coil," that the now undeveloped, the half dormant powers, that mysteriously sleep within it, may awake to their own intellectual and immortal life. It may be as unconscious now of what it is hereafter to become, as the reptile that crawls upon the earth is of rising to the air and light of heaven. The transformation may be as great, and as much more glorious, as intellect is more glorious than dark and blind instinct. Nor may death be the soul's last transformation. "There shall be no more death," indeed; but there may be many changes in its mode of being, while it is passing from glory to glory, through its everlasting progress.

But we must not delay longer to consider some of those views of death, which are indeed more just than those already noticed, but which nevertheless are liable to be wrested into error, through the excessive dread which is entertained of this event. Mortality is not the interruption of being, nor is it any peculiar visitation of God's wrath; but it is still a serious crisis in our existence; and our views of it are not likely to be too serious, if we will only guard our seriousness from superstition, and from all irrational and extravagant influences of the imagination.

Death is a serious event, inasmuch as we are taught that "after death is the judgment." Men may do wrong now, and boast of it, may purpose evil and glory in its accomplishment, may oppress and injure, and silence the voice of remonstrance; but an hour of unveiled retribution is approaching them; the time is near when every evil gratification and unjust deed shall become a piercing arrow of conviction. Forms, appearances, shall soon give place to realities; the body's enslaving control, to the spirit's action and life; and passion, indulgence, sin, to the manifested and the no longer mistaken judgment of Heaven.

Still however, solemn and justly solemn as this view of death and of the revelation of a future life is, it is possible to lay too great, or at least too exclusive, a stress upon that event which is to unfold to us those revelations. Every future moment —not that of death only, not that of the judgment which is immediately to follow —but every future moment of our being is to answer for every present moment. This is the great law of retribution. None less strict, or less severe, belongs to our moral nature. And it does not apply to the future life only, but equally to the present; and all the difference is, that it is now less clearly seen and felt. And it does not apply to any one epoch alone, but to all the periods, to all the moments of our endless being. It is not death then that we should fear, but the eternal retribution of conscience. It is not at the moment of death that we should tremble, but at every moment of the future that is to answer for the neglects, and errors, and offences of the misspent past. Virtue is deathless. It is more; it is blessed life. On the "path of the just, that shineth brighter and brighter," no shadow abideth. The shade of death itself but opens the way to a brighter and more glorious existence.

Again; death is the separation of friends. And we are not of those who can speak lightly of this separation. We have heard of some who were able to lift up a radiant and almost smiling countenance over the earthly remains of all that was dearest on earth; but it enters not into our conception to regard it as any thing but extravagance and enthusiasm. We do not take upon us to set limits to the support which God may give to bereaved friendship or afflicted piety; but that triumph in the countenance, surely, is not their fit demeanor. No; the sundering stroke of death is stern, and cold, and bitter reality.

We have sometimes ventured to wonder, and that in the more fervent meditation upon God's goodness, why the trial is made so severe, and for a time so almost inconsolable. Could one glimpse, we have been ready to say, could one glimpse of the future world be opened to us, could the situation of the departed for one moment be made known to us; or might it have been the order of Providence that families should be removed at once and together to the "spirit land"—but reflection and faith have soon arisen to check the remonstrances and questionings of anxious and yearning affection, and have soon shown, as they usually do, that God's providence is wiser than our own hasty presumption. Were families removed together, how certainly would our social affections gather up and concentrate themselves upon those narrow circles; and all the evils—the peculiarities, the prejudices, the selfish and exclusive attachments—of that limited intercourse, to which we are already sufficiently liable, would be inflicted on society; and all the benefits of a wide and generous diffusion and reciprocation of sentiments and feelings would be cut off from the social body. If, again, the future world were opened to us, it might produce in us an utter distaste to this; it might disturb the well balanced and wisely ordered influences, under which we were made to act in the present state. If we could see, what we so ardently long to behold, beyond this veil of earthly shadows, we might have no eyes for the scene around us; we might be rapt in meditation, when we are called to the action and trial of all our virtues.

It was evidently designed, that we should be trained up here, by a severe and lofty discipline, for some glorious state of being and enjoyment hereafter. The moral economy under which we are placed, the spiritual life on earth, was not designed to be vision, but faith,—not rapture, but trial. The departure of friends and kindred to another world irresistibly draws our thoughts thither, and constantly renders us more indifferent to acquisitions and objects here. Heaven claims our treasures, that our hearts may be there also. Faith, moreover, in the invisible, the spiritual, the eternal, is the appropriate faith of beings whose welfare lies in the invisible mind, whose nature is spiritual, and whose destiny immortal. It is meet that we should be trained by the influences of a world which we see not, and from which no sound reaches us. It is our happiness, also, not only to love God, but to love him with the fervor and assurance of perfect trust. Love is ever doubtful, without that trial—and it is but an impassioned feeling without that quality—of absolute confidence.

Yet a little while therefore are we required to wait, till we can behold those objects and those beings on whom, next to God, it is right that our hearts should be set. The interval will not be too long for the trial of our faith, and the preparation of all our virtues; not too long to prepare us for the blessedness of a future life; nay, it may not be found too long to prepare us *to die*, as the Christian should die. To meet the last hour calmly, to resign all the objects which our senses have made familiar and dear, in the lofty expectation of better things for the mind, is itself a great act of faith, and one for which many days' reflection and experience may not be too much to prepare us. To take our last look at the countenances of beloved friends and companions; to close our eyes to the bright vision of nature; to bid adieu to earth, sky, waters; to feel, for the last time, the thrill of rapture with which this fair and glorious scene of things has so often touched the soul—this is an hour for faith unshaken in the immortality of virtue, and for trust unbounded in the love of God, and for the triumphant assurance which long tried and lofty experience alone can give. The feelings of the infidel Rousseau have seemed to us thus far natural, and such as even a Christian may entertain. When he apprehended that his last hour drew near, he desired the windows of his apartment to be opened, that he might "have the pleasure," as he said, "of beholding nature once more. How lovely she is!" he exclaimed; "how pure and serene is the day! O Nature! thou art grand indeed!" Yet not as Rousseau died does the Christian die; but with a better trust.

And with that trust, with a firm confidence in the perpetuity of all pious and virtuous friendships, there is much, surely, to mitigate the pain of a temporary separation. Let us remember, too, that we do submit to frequent separations in this life, that our friends wander from us over trackless waters and to far distant continents, and that we are still happy in the assurance that they live. And though, by the same providence of God that has guarded them here, they are called to pass beyond the visible precincts of this present existence, let us feel that they still live. God's universe is not explored when we have surveyed islands, and oceans, and the shores of earth's spreading continents. There are other regions, where the footsteps of the happy and immortal are treading the paths of life. Would we call them back to these abodes of infirmity and sin? Would we involve them again in these toils, and pains, and temptations? Or shall we sorrow for them as those who have no hope? No; we would rather go and die with them. What do we say? We will rather go and live with them forever!

But, the awful entrance to the world of spirits—may still be our exclamation—how dark and desolate is that passage! It is a fearful thing to die. Nature abhors dissolution.

Let something of this be admitted, but

let it not be too much. Does nature abhor dissolution? Behold the signs of decay and dissolution which the season now spreads around us. Behold nature in her annual death—the precursor of renovated life. But we will not argue from emblems. We will admit that a living being must naturally dread to part with life. But he dreads to part with life, only in a greater measure, as he dreads to part with every thing that is his. He is averse to the loss of property, and in some instances almost as much so as to the loss of life itself. He is reluctant to part with any one of his senses; and this reluctance, compared with the natural dread of death, is in full proportion to the value of that organ. Let us rationally look at the subject in this light. Doubtless we dread the loss of the sense of hearing, for instance; and, when that is entirely gone from us, hearing is dead. We dread the loss of sight; and, that light extinguished, seeing is dead. Thus one faculty after another departs from us, and death is at work within us, while we say that we are in the midst of life. So let us regard it. So let us familiarize to our minds the thoughts of death, and feel that this dreaded enemy, dreaded partly because imagined to be so distant and unknown, has already made its lodgment in our frame, and by familiar processes is approaching the citadel of life. As disease is making its inroads upon us and the system is wearing out, as the acuteness of sensation is failing us, and the vigor of bone and muscle is declining, let us say and feel, that we are gradually approaching the extinction of this animal life. Let no sceptic doubts, let no thoughts of annihilation mingle with our apprehensions of mortality; let us believe as Christians, that not the soul, but only the body dies—and death cannot be that dread and abhorrence of nature which we make it.

We would dwell upon this point a moment longer—the natural dread of death. It seems to us strange, it seems as if all were wrong, in a world, where from the very constitution of things death must close every scene of human life, where it has reigned for ages over all generations, where the very air we breathe and the dust we tread upon was once animated life—it seems to us most strange and wrong, that this most common, necessary, expedient, and certain of all events should bring such horror and desolation with it; that it should bring such tremendous agitation, as if it were some awful and unprecedented phenomenon; that it should be more than death—a shock, a catastrophe, a convulsion; as if nature, instead of holding on its steady course, were falling into irretrievable ruins.

And that which is strange, is our strangeness to this event. Call sickness, call pain, an approach to death. Call the weariness and failure of the limbs and senses, call decay, a dying. It is so; it is a gradual loosening of the cords of life, and a breaking up of its reservoirs and resources. So shall they all, one and another in succession, give way. "I feel"—will the thoughtful man say—"I feel the pang of suffering, as it were, piercing and cutting asunder, one by one, the fine and invisible bonds that hold me to the earth. I feel the gushing current of life within me to be wearing away its own channels. I feel the sharpness of every keen emotion and of every acute and far-penetrating thought, as if it were shortening the moments of the soul's connexion and conflict with the body." So it is, and so shall it be, till at last "the silver cord is loosened, and the golden bowl is broken, and the pitcher is broken at the fountain, and the wheel is broken at the cistern, and the dust returns to the earth as it was, and the spirit returns unto God who gave it."

No; it is not a strange dispensation. Death is the fellow of all that is earthly; the friend of man alone. It is not an anomaly; it is not a monster in the creation. It is the law and the lot of nature.

"Not to thy eternal resting-place
Shalt thou retire alone. * * *

Thou shalt lie down
With patriarchs of the infant world, with kings,
The powerful of the earth, the wise and good,
Fair forms and hoary seers of ages past,
All in one mighty sepulchre. The hills,
Rock-ribbed and ancient as the sun; the vales,
Stretching in pensive quietness between;
The venerable woods, rivers that move
In majesty, and the complaining brooks,
That make the meadows green, and, poured round all,
Old ocean's gray and melancholy waste—
Are but the solemn decorations all
Of the great tomb of man."

But of what is it the tomb? Does the spirit die? Do the blessed affections of the soul go down into the dark and silent grave? Oh! no. "The narrow house, and pall, and breathless darkness" and funereal train—these belong not to the soul. They proclaim only the body's dissolution. They but celebrate the vanishing away of the shadow of existence. Man does not die, though the forms of popular speech thus announce his exit. He does not die. We bury, not our friend, but only the form, the vehicle in which for a time our friend lived. That cold, impassive clay is not the friend, the parent, the child, the companion, the cherished being. No, it is not: blessed be God, that we can say, *It is not!* It is the material mould only that earth claims. It is "dust," only, that "descends to dust." The grave! let us break its awful spell, its dread dominion. It is the place where man lays down his weakness, his infirmity, his diseases and sorrows, that he may rise up to a new and glorious life. It is the place where man ceases—in all that is frail and decaying—ceases to be man, that he may be, in glory and blessedness, an angel of light!

Why, then, should we fear death, save as the wicked fear, and must fear it? Why dread to lay down this frail body in its resting-place, and this weary, aching head on the pillow of its repose? Why tremble at this—that in the long sleep of the tomb that body shall suffer disease no more, and pain no more, and hear no more the cries of want nor the groans of distress—and, far retired from the turmoil of life, that violence and change shall pass lightly over it, and the elements shall beat and the storms shall sigh unheard around its lowly bed? Say, ye aged and infirm! is it the greatest of evils to die? Say, ye children of care and toil! say, ye afflicted and tempted! is it the greatest of evils to die?

Oh! no. Come the last hour, in God's own time!—and a good life and a glorious hope shall make it welcome. Come the hour of release!—and affliction shall make it welcome. Come the hour of reunion with the loved and lost on earth!—and the passionate yearnings of affection, and the strong aspiration of faith, shall bear us to their blessed land. Come death to this body—this burdened, tempted, frail, failing, dying body!—and to the soul,—thanks be to God who giveth us the victory,—to the soul come freedom, light and joy unceasing! come the immortal life! "He that liveth"—saith the Conqueror over death—"he that liveth and believeth in me shall NEVER DIE!"

THE DEPARTED.

The friends we love have passed away;
  The forms so dear no more we see;
No more we meet the eye's mild ray,
  Or catch the smile of sympathy.

No—these are fled; but ask thy heart,
  Are no fond traces lingering there,—
Memories we would not bid depart,
  And hopes that bless our hour of prayer?

Is not the dream of heaven more sweet,
  Bright with the living forms of love?
Does not each trial that we meet
  Raise our rapt spirits more above?

Yes! death, that pales our curdling cheek,
  Tells of an angel's opening bliss—
Again we view the form we seek,
  Bright with immortal happiness.

For faith delighted views that scene
  Of fadeless glory and of grace,
Forgets the years that intervene,
  And bids us see them "face to face."

What though a few brief ills of life,
  A little pathway marked with tears,
Some struggles of the Christian strife
  Await us in those future years;—

Soon, soon they pass; and even now
  Those angel forms may guard our way,
Weave the blest chaplet for our brow,
  And guide our footsteps lest they stray.

In every thought to heaven allied,
  In every virtuous deed and aim,
Are the departed at our side,
  Whose memory fans the sacred flame.

And is this death? first born to God,
  To trace that pure celestial sphere,
And rise in faith and hope unawed,
  To joys we scarce can vision here?

Oh early blest—how vain our sighs,
  Our fond, impetuous tears how vain;
To heaven we raise our weeping eyes—
  Our loss is their eternal gain.

DEATH AND SLEEP.

The angel of sleep and the angel of death were journeying arm in arm on the earth. Evening drew on. They seated themselves on a hill not far from the habitations of men. A solemn silence reigned around, and the evening bell in the distant village ceased to be heard.

Tranquil and silent as it is their nature to be, these two benefactors of mortals sat in fraternal embrace, and night already approached.

The angel of sleep then rose from his mossy seat, and strewed with delicate hand the invisible germs of slumber. The evening breezes wafted them to the peaceful habitations of the weary husbandmen. Sweet slumbers now fell upon the inmates of the rustic dwellings, from the aged, whose tottering steps are supported by a staff, to the infant in the cradle. The sick forgot their pains, the afflicted their sorrows, and poverty its cares. All eyes were closed.

Having performed his task, the kindly angel of sleep resumed his seat beside his graver brother. When the morning dawn awakes, cried he with joyous innocence, then will men praise me as their friend and benefactor! O how delightful to do good secretly and unseen! How happy are we invisible ministers of the Most High! How pleasing the silent duty which we are charged to perform!

Thus spake the benevolent angel of sleep.

The angel of death surveyed him with silent melancholy, and tears, such as immortals weep, started into his large dark eyes. Ah! said he, why am I not destined, like thee, to receive the tribute of joyful gratitude? Mortals regard me as their enemy and the destroyer of their pleasures.

Oh, my brother, replied the angel of sleep, will not the good, when they awake, acknowledge and thankfully bless thee as their friend and benefactor? Are not we brothers and servants of one Father?

He spoke, and the eyes of the angel of death glistened, and the brother spirits clasped each other in a tender embrace.

IMMORTALITY.

Oh, never shall my soul the thoughts forego,
  Of high and pure intent, that lead me on
  To virtue's heights, and the immortal crown,
Wreathed of the flowers that in heaven's garden grow.
What though I tread a path of tears and woe,
  Nor mortal joy attendant on my way,
  The light of hope shall 'mid the darkness play
And purer pleasures teach my heart to glow.
I long to join the blissful band on high,
  The spirits of the just, who overcame
  The bonds of sin, and whose undying fame
Shall guide me to their glorious destiny.
Then shrink not, Oh my soul! but undismayed,
Seek for the crown of life which will not fade.

TRUST IN GOD UNDER AFFLICTIONS.

Numberless are the afflictions in body, mind, or fortune to which we are liable, and under which mankind are continually suffering. While some are complaining of their losses, others are lamenting their successes. While some are mourning over dead relatives, others are mourning over living ones. One was lately happy in a companion and friend,—a wife perhaps, a husband, or a child, who was the comfort and delight of his life, but who has been torn from him by the stroke of death. He is left alone to travel the journey of life; he recollects with anguish the happiness he has lost, and a black veil is spread over all his enjoyments. Another has met with disappointments in his pursuits, or misfortunes in business; he has been crossed in his hopes, and has miscarried in his undertakings; he is sunk under difficulties, and reduced from ease and plenty and affluence to perplexity and poverty. One is languishing under a fatal distemper,—his strength exhausted, and his spirits broken; the capacity of enjoying pleasure gone, the king of terrors threatening him, and the dreary grave opening to receive him. Another is pining away in a deep melancholy, terrified by apprehensions of imaginary evils, a stranger to every cheerful thought, anxious and distressed he knows not why, every object about him thrown into a dismal shade, and his whole soul wrapped up in darkness and horror.

In such circumstances we are necessarily led to look out for comfort. Our condition would be dismal indeed had we nothing to stay our minds upon, or no cheering reflections to make in a time of private or public distress, when perhaps all the help of man is vain. But this is not our case. There is an anchor of hope, on which we may always rely when tossed on the tempestuous sea of this world. There is a fund of consolation, to which we may always have recourse amidst the calamities to which we are liable. I mean, "trusting in the name of the Lord, and staying ourselves upon God." Are then any of us dejected or unhappy? Is our prospect darkened by any cloud, or are we discouraged by the prospect of impending evil? Let us turn our thoughts to the Deity, and reflect on his perfect government. Let us consider that the Lord reigneth, and that his righteous Providence directs all events; and that we cannot suffer except by the will of a wise and faithful Creator. This will throw a bright light into our minds, and give us relief and support in all circumstances.

In order to be more explicit here, I would observe, first, that in such circumstances we should consider, that the Deity is always intimately present with us, and sees all that passes in the world. It is his constant influence that preserves the world, and were he to withdraw his hand, or to suspend his energy, all nature would fall to pieces. He cannot, therefore, be unacquainted with any thing we feel or fear. He is indeed one with our souls; the first mover in every motion, and the animating principle which gives efficacy to all the powers of nature.

In times of darkness it is proper we should further consider that this Being who is continually present with us, stands in the nearest relation to us. He is our parent,—we are his offspring. He is our maker,—we are his creatures; and it is impossible there should be a nearer relation than that of children to their parent, or of creatures to their Creator. From Him we derive all our faculties,—to Him we owe all we possess; the world is the work of his hands, and through and to Him are all things.

To these reflections, let us add that this Being, thus present with us, and thus related to us, is almighty, all-wise, and all-benevolent. Infinite power, wisdom, and goodness form one idea, and are necessarily united in the first Cause. There is no truth so important as this. It throws a lustre on every object, and is enough to reconcile us to every event. It is confirmed by the voice and testimony of all nature. Wherever we see power displayed, there we see benevolence displayed.

Nothing can afford such a ground for consolation in seasons of darkness, as the reflection on which I am now insisting. It gives a stay for our minds which can never fail or disappoint us. The immediate and necessary inference from it is, that we cannot possibly fall into any distress, or suffer any evil, which it is unfit we should suffer. This is just as certain as that there is a Deity who is present with us, and knows what we suffer; that he is our Maker, and cannot see what we suffer with indifference; that he is omnipotent, and able to remove it—infinitely good, and inclined to remove it.

Remember this, whenever any afflictions threaten you. Look up then to the first Cause, and consider that his goodness cannot but chase out of nature every calamity as soon as it becomes needless or improper.

My feelings have been sometimes so shocked when I have seen a fellow-creature groaning under distress, that I have been ready to cry out in my haste, "How is it possible that such sufferings should be consistent with the goodness of the Deity?" But I have soon corrected myself by considering, whence did I receive these feelings? Can I be more compassionate than the Being who gave me my compassion? Were he malevolent, would he have made me to detest malevolence? Is it credible that he should have planted within me principles which render his own character shocking to me? Let us then in every season of private trouble, or public calamity, "trust in the name of the Lord, and stay ourselves upon God." We exist not in a forlorn or fatherless world. We are the care and charge of infinite wisdom. All is well in nature, and every event subject to the best superintendency. We can wish for nothing beyond this. In such circumstances, to repine and mourn would be folly intolerable. It would be to repine and mourn because the world is not governed according to our narrow views; that is, because it is not governed wrong. Could we work into our hearts these convictions, or bring ourselves properly under their power, we should receive every affliction as a blessing; and in the midst of a storm or convulsion that may overturn a kingdom, we should hear a voice whispering peace to us, and assuring us of a favorable and happy issue. In short, knowing that every circumstance in the constitution of the world, and the administration of events, is right beyond a possibility of correction, and good beyond a possibility of improvement, we should at all times take up the words of the prophet Habakkuk, "although the fig-tree should not blossom, or fruit be in the vine, though the labor of the olive should fail, and the fields yield no meat, and the flock be cut off from the fold, and there should be no herd in the stall; yet I will rejoice in the Lord, and glory in the God of my salvation."

I cannot help observing here particularly, that our confidence in the Deity ought to be implicit; and that no appearances of irregularity in the dispensations of his providence ought to have any tendency to destroy it. Such appearances are unavoidable to creatures who see but a part of the plan of Providence, and who are such incompetent judges of it as we are. There could not indeed be a stronger objection to it than our finding it so level to our capacities, that nothing in it appeared to us irregular or mysterious. This would be a greater difficulty than any that now occurs to us in contemplating God's government. It would imply, that the world was established, and that the course of events is directed by a wisdom no higher than our own.

In examining the works of a complete artist, do you ever expect to understand the propriety and beaüty of every part of it? In order to this, ought you not yourself to be a complete artist? In reading a learned book, do you not always reckon the obscurer parts to be of a piece with the other parts, and not conclude them to be nonsense, because you do not understand them? In considering also the measures of any human government, do we not always reckon the same kind of allowance for our own ignorance to be reasonable? In the present instance there is infinitely more reason for making such an allowance; for we are infinitely less qualified to judge of the works of God and the scheme of Providence, than the lowest of us are to judge of the measures of the best-conducted government.

It is necessary I should add, that all the encouragements on which I have now insisted are confirmed and increased by the Christian revelation. The arguments I have offered prove that we may assuredly expect an exemption from every evil that it is improper we should suffer, and the possession of every good that it is proper we should enjoy. The voice of revelation concurs with reason in giving us this expectation. Christianity teaches us, that "not a sparrow falls to the ground without our heavenly Father,—that the hairs of our head are all numbered by Him,—that his tender mercies are over all his works,—that He never willingly grieveth any of us,—that afflictions are sent by Him for our correction and improvement,—that He only is wise and righteous, and at the same time in such a degree that it may be justly said that there is none besides good,—and that, in particular, He has displayed his goodness to us in sending Christ, the great Messiah, into the world to reveal his will to us, to deliver us from death, and to bring us to a blessed and glorious immortality." This is an information which raises our hopes to infinity; and under the influence of this hope we are exhorted to rejoice evermore, in every thing to give thanks, and to welcome tribulation as working for us an exceeding and eternal weight of glory.

The language which the Scriptures direct us to adopt in times of darkness is such language as the following: "When my soul fainteth I will remember the Lord; He is my light and my refuge, therefore will I not fear, though the earth be removed and the mountains be carried into the midst of the sea. O Lord of hosts, blessed is the man that trusteth in Thee; he shall not be afraid of the terror by night, or the arrow that flieth by day; no evil shall befall him, neither shall any plague come nigh his dwelling."

FILIAL TRUST

My Father! when around me spread
  I see the shadows of the tomb,
And life's bright visions droop and fade,
  And darkness veils my future doom;

Oh, in that anguished hour I turn
  With a still trusting heart to thee!

And holy thoughts still shine and burn
  Amid that cold, sad destiny.

They fill my soul with heavenly light,
  While all around is pain and woe;
And strengthened by them in thy sight,
  Father, to drink thy cup I go!

Thy will be done—I will not fear
  The fate provided by thy love;
Though clouds and darkness shroud me here,
  I know that all is bright above.

The stars of heaven are shining on,
  Though these frail eyes are dim with tears;
The hopes of earth indeed are gone,
  But are not ours th' immortal years?

Father! forgive the heart that clings
  Thus trembling to the things of time,
And bid my soul on angel wings
  Ascend into a purer clime!

There shall no doubts disturb its trust,
  No sorrows dim celestial love;
But these afflictions of the dust,
  Like shadows of the night, remove.

That glorious hour will well repay
  A life of toil, and care, and woe;
Oh Father! joyful on my way,
  To drink thy bitter cup I go!

THE FUTURE LIFE.

There is one method in which Christ's resurrection gives aid to our faith in another life, which is not often dwelt on, and which seems to me worthy of attention. Our chief doubts and difficulties in regard to that state spring chiefly from the senses and the imagination, and not from the reason. The eye fixed on the lifeless body, on the wan features and the motionless limbs, and the imagination following the frame into the dark tomb, and representing to itself the stages of decay and ruin, are apt to fill and oppress the mind with discouraging and appalling thoughts. The senses can detect in the pale corpse not a trace of the activity of that spirit which lately moved it. Death seems to have achieved an entire victory;

and when reason and revelation speak of continued and a higher life, the senses and imagination, pointing to the disfigured and mouldering body, obscure by their sad forebodings the light which reason and revelation strive to kindle in the bereaved soul.

Now the resurrection of Christ meets, if I may so say, the senses and imagination on their own ground, contends with them with their own weapons. It shows us the very frame on which death in its most humiliating form had set its seal, and which had been committed in utter hopelessness to the tomb, rising, breathing, moving with new life; and rising not to return again to the earth, but, after a short sojourn, to ascend from the earth to a purer region, and thus to attest man's destination to a higher life. These facts, submitted to the very senses, and almost necessarily kindling the imagination to explore the unseen world, seem to me particularly suited to overcome the main difficulties in the way of Christian faith.

Reason is not left to struggle alone with the horrors of the tomb. The assurance that Jesus Christ, who lived on the earth, who died on the cross, and was committed a mutilated, bleeding frame to the receptacle of the dead, rose uninjured, and then exchanged an earthly for a heavenly life, puts to flight the said auguries which rise like spectres from the grave, and helps us to conceive, as in our present weakness we could not otherwise conceive, of man's appointed triumph over death.

Such is one of the aids given by the resurrection to faith in immortality. Still this faith is lamentably weak in the multitude of men. To multitudes heaven is almost a world of fancy. It wants substance. The idea of a world in which beings exist without these gross bodies, exist as pure spirits, or clothed with refined and spiritual frames, strikes them as a fiction. What cannot be seen or touched, appears unreal. This is mournful but not wonderful; for how can men, who immerse themselves in the body and its in terests, and cultivate no acquaintance with their own souls and spiritual powers, comprehend a higher, spiritual life? There are multitudes who pronounce a man a visionary, who speaks distinctly and joyfully of his future being, and of the triumph of the mind over bodily decay.

This scepticism as to things spiritual and celestial, is as irrational and unphilosophical as it is degrading. We have more evidence that we have souls or spirits than that we have bodies. We are surer that we think, and feel, and will, than that we have solid and extended limbs and organs. Philosophers have said much to disprove the existence of matter and motion, but they have not tried to disprove the existence of thought; for it is by thought that they attempt to set aside the reality of material nature.

Farther; how irrational is it to imagine that there are no worlds but this, and no higher modes of existence than our own. Who that sends his eye through this immense creation, can doubt that there are orders of beings superior to ourselves, or can see any thing unreasonable in the doctrine, that there are states in which mind exists less circumscribed and clogged by matter than on earth; in other words, that there is a spiritual world? It is childish to make this infant life of ours the model of existence in all other worlds. The philosopher, especially, who sees a vast chain of beings and an infinite variety of life on this single globe, which is but a point in creation, should be ashamed of that narrowness of mind which can anticipate nothing nobler in the universe of God than his present mode of being.

How, now, shall the doctrine of a future, higher life, the doctrine both of reason and revelation, be brought to bear more powerfully on the mind, to become more real and effectual? Various methods might be given. I shall confine myself to one. This method is, to seek some clearer, more definite conception of the future state. That world seems less real for want of some distinctness in its features. We should all believe it more firmly if we conceived of it more vividly. It seems unsubstantial from its vagueness and dimness. I think it right, then, to use the aids of Scripture and reason in forming to ourselves something like a sketch of the life to come. The Scriptures, indeed, give not many materials for such a delineation, but the few they furnish are invaluable, especially when we add to these the lights thrown over futurity by the knowledge of our own spiritual nature. Every new law of the mind which we discover helps us to comprehend its destiny; for its future life must correspond to its great laws and essential powers.

These aids we should employ to give distinctness to the spiritual state; and it is particularly useful so to do, when excellent beings, whom we have known and loved, pass from earth into that world. Nature prompts us to follow them to their new abode, to inquire into their new life, to represent to ourselves their new happiness; and perhaps the spiritual world never becomes so near and real to us, as when we follow into it dear friends, and sympathize with them in the improvements and enjoyments of that blessed life. Do not say that there is danger here of substituting imagination for truth. There is no danger if we confine ourselves to the spiritual views of heaven given us in the New Testament, and interpret these by the principles and powers of our own souls. To me the subject is too dear and sacred to allow me to indulge myself in dreams. I want reality; I want truth; and this I find in God's word and in the human soul.

When our virtuous friends leave the world, we know not the place where they go. We can turn our eyes to no spot in the universe and say they are there. Nor is our ignorance here of any moment. It is unimportant what region of space contains them. Whilst we know not to what place they go, we know, what is infinitely more interesting, to what beings they go.

We know not where heaven is, but we know whom it contains, and this knowledge opens us an infinite field for contemplation and delight.

Our virtuous friends at death go to Jesus Christ. The New Testament always speaks of Jesus as existing now in the spiritual world, and Paul tells us that it is the happiness of the holy, when absent from the body, to be present with the Lord. Here is one great fact in regard to futurity. The good, on leaving us here, meet their Savior; and this view alone assures us of their unutterable happiness. In this world they had cherished acquaintance with Jesus through the records of the Evangelists. They had followed him through his eventful life with veneration and love, had treasured in their memories his words, works, and life-giving promises, and by receiving his spirit had learned something of the virtues and happiness of a higher world. Now they meet him, they see him. He is no longer a faint object to their mind, obscured by distance and by the mists of sense and the world. He is present to them, and more intimately present than we are to each other. Of this we are sure; for whilst the precise mode of our future existence is unknown, we do know that spiritual beings in that higher state must approach and commune with each other more and more intimately in proportion to their progress. Those who are newly born into heaven meet Jesus, and meet from him the kindest welcome. The happiness of the Savior, in receiving to a higher life a human being who has been redeemed, purified, inspired with immortal goodness by his influence, we can but imperfectly comprehend. You can conceive what would be your feelings on welcoming to shore your best friend, who had been tossed on a perilous sea; but the raptures of earthly reunion are faint compared with the happiness of Jesus in receiving the spirit for which he died, and which under his guidance has passed with an improving virtue through a world of sore temptation. We on earth meet after our long separations to suffer as well as enjoy, and soon to part again. Jesus meets those who ascend from earth to heaven with the consciousness that their trial is past, their race is run, that death is conquered. With his far-reaching, prophetic eye he sees them entering a career of joy and glory never to end. And his benevolent welcome is expressed with a power which belongs only to the utterance of heaven, and which communicates to them an immediate, confiding, overflowing joy. You know that on earth we sometimes meet human beings whose countenances at the first view scatter all distrust, and win from us something like the reliance of a long-tried friendship. One smile is enough to let us into their hearts, to reveal to us a goodness on which we may repose. That smile with which Jesus will meet the new-born inhabitant of heaven, that joyful greeting, that beaming of love from him who bled for us, that tone of welcome,—all these I can faintly conceive, but no language can utter them. The joys of centuries will be crowded into that meeting. This is not fiction. It is truth founded on the essential laws of the mind.

Our friends, when they enter heaven, meet Jesus Christ, and their intercourse with him will be of the most affectionate and ennobling character. There will be nothing of distance in it. Jesus is indeed sometimes spoken of as reigning in the future world, and sometimes imagination places him on a real and elevated throne. Strange that such conceptions can enter the minds of Christians. Jesus will indeed reign in heaven, and so he reigned on earth. He reigned in the fishing boat, from which he taught; in the humble dwelling, where he gathered round him listening and confiding disciples. His reign is not the vulgar dominion of this world. It is the empire of a great, godlike, disinterested being, over minds capable of comprehending and loving him. In heaven nothing like what we call government on earth can exist, for government here is founded in human weakness and guilt. The voice of command is never heard among the spirits of the just. Even on earth the most perfect government is that of a family, where parents employ no tone but that of affectionate counsel, where filial affection reads its duty in the mild look and finds its law and motive in its own pure impulse. Christ will not be raised on a throne above his followers. On earth he sat at the same table with the publican and sinner. Will he recede from the excellent whom he has fitted for celestial mansions? How minds will communicate with one another in that world, we know not; but we know that our closest embraces are but types of the spiritual nearness which will then be enjoyed; and to this intimacy with Jesus the new-born inhabitant of heaven is admitted.

But we have not yet exhausted this source of future happiness. The excellent go from earth not only to receive a joyful welcome and assurances of eternal love from the Lord. There is a still higher view. They are brought by this new intercourse to a new comprehension of his mind, and to a new reception of his spirit. It is indeed a happiness to know that we are objects of interest and love to an illustrious being; but it is a greater happiness to know deeply the sublime and beautiful character of this being, to sympathize with him, to enter into his vast thoughts and pure designs, and to become associated with him in the great ends for which he lives. Even here in our infant and dim state of being we learn enough of Jesus, of his divine philanthropy triumphant over injuries and agonies, to thrill us with affectionate admiration. But those in heaven look into that vast, godlike soul as we have never done. They approach it as we cannot approach the soul of the most confiding friend; and this nearness to the mind of Jesus awakens in themselves a power of love and virtue, which they little suspected during their earthly being. We all know how a man of mighty genius and of heroic feeling can impart himself to other minds, and raise them for a time to something like his own energy; and in this we have a faint delineation of the power to be exerted on the minds of those who approach Jesus after death. As nature springs to a new life under the beams of the sun, so will the human soul be warmed and expanded under the influence of Jesus Christ. It will then become truly conscious of the immortal power treasured up in itself. His greatness will not overwhelm it, but will awaken a corresponding grandeur.

Nor is this topic yet exhausted. The good, on approaching Jesus, will not only sympathize with his spirit, but will become joint workers, active, efficient ministers, in accomplishing his great work of spreading virtue and happiness. We must never think of heaven as a state of inactive contemplation, or of unproductive feeling. Even here on earth, the influence of Christ's character is seen in awakening an active, self-sacrificing goodness. It sends the true disciples to the abodes of the suffering. It binds them by new ties to their race. It gives them a new consciousness of being created for a ministry of beneficence; and can they, when they approach more nearly this divine Philanthropist, and learn, by a new alliance with him, the fullness of his love, can they fail to consecrate themselves to his work and to kindred labors with an energy of will unknown on earth? In truth, our sympathy with Christ could not be perfect, did we not act with him. Nothing so unites beings as co-operation in the same glorious cause, and to this union with Christ the excellent above are received.

There is another very interesting view of the future state, which seems to me to be a necessary consequence of the connection to be formed there with Jesus Christ. Those who go there from among us must retain the deepest interest in this world. Their ties to those they have left are not dissolved, but only refined. On this point, indeed, I want not the evidence of revelation; I want no other evidence than the essential principles and laws of the soul. If the future state is to be an improvement on the present, if intellect is to be invigorated and love expanded there, then memory, the fundamental power of the intellect, must act with new energy on the past, and all the benevolent affections which have been cherished here must be quickened into a higher life. To suppose the present state blotted out hereafter from the mind, would be to destroy its use, would cut off all connection between the two worlds, and would subvert responsibility; for how can retribution be awarded for a forgotten existence? No; we must carry the present with us, whether we enter the world of happiness or woe. The good will indeed form new, holier, stronger ties above; but under the expanding influence of that better world the human heart will be capacious enough to retain the old whilst it receives the new, to remember its birthplace with tenderness whilst enjoying a maturer and happier being. Did I think of those who are gone as dying to those they left, I should honor and love them less. The man who forgets his home when he quits it, seems to want the best sensibilities of our nature; and if the good were to forget their brethren on earth in their new abode, were to cease to intercede for them in their nearer approach to their common Father, could we think of them as improved by the change?

All this I am compelled to infer from the nature of the human mind. But when I add to this, that the new-born heirs of heaven go to Jesus Christ, the great lover of the human family, who dwelt here, suffered here, who moistened our earth with his tears and blood, who has gone not to break off, but to continue and perfect his beneficent labors for mankind, whose mind never for a moment turns from our race, whose interest in the progress of his truth and the salvation of the tempted soul has been growing more and more intense ever since he left our world, and who has thus bound up our race with his very being,—when I think of all this, I am sure that they cannot forget our world. Could we hear them, I believe they would tell us that they never truly loved the race before; never before knew what it is to sympathize with human sorrow, to rejoice in human virtue, to mourn for human guilt. A new fountain of love to man is opened within them. They now see what before dimly gleamed on them, the capacities, the mysteries of a human soul. The significance of that word Immortality is now apprehended, and every being destined to it rises into unutterable importance. They love human nature as never before, and human friends are prized as above all price.

Perhaps it may be asked whether those born into heaven not only remember with interest, but have a present, immediate knowledge of those whom they left on earth. On this point neither Scripture nor the principles of human nature give us light, and we are of course left to uncertainty. I will only say, that I know nothing to prevent such knowledge. We are indeed accustomed to think of heaven as distant; but of this we have no proof. Heaven is the union, the society of spiritual, higher beings. May not these fill the universe, so as to make heaven everywhere? are such beings probably circumscribed, as we are, by material limits? Milton has said,—

> "Millions of spiritual beings walk the earth
> Both when we wake and when we sleep."

It is possible that the distance of heaven lies wholly in the veil of flesh, which we now want power to penetrate. A new sense, a new eye, might show the spiritual world compassing us on every side.

But suppose heaven to be remote. Still we on earth may be visible to its inhabitants; still in an important sense they may be present; for what do we mean by presence? Am I not present to those of you who are beyond the reach of my arm, but whom I distinctly see? And is it at all inconsistent with our knowledge of nature, to suppose that those in heaven, whatever be their abode, may have spiritual senses, organs by which they may discern the remote as clearly as we do the near? This little ball of sight can see the planets at the distance of millions of miles, and by the aids of science can distinguish the inequalities of their surfaces. And it is easy for us to conceive of an organ of vision so sensitive and piercing, that from our earth the inhabitants of those far-rolling worlds might be discerned. Why then may not they who have entered a higher state, and are clothed with spiritual frames, survey our earth as distinctly as when it was their abode?

This may be the truth; but if we receive it as such, let us not abuse it. It is liable to abuse. Let us not think of the departed as looking on us with earthly, partial affections. They love us more than ever, but with a refined and spiritual love. They have now but one wish for us, which is, that we may fit ourselves to join them in their mansions of benevolence and piety. Their spiritual vision penetrates to our souls. Could we hear their voice, it would not be an utterance of personal attachment, so much as a quickening call to greater effort, to more resolute self-denial, to a wider charity, to a meeker endurance, a more filial obedience of the will of God. Nor must we think of them as appropriated to ourselves. They are breathing now an atmosphere of divine benevolence. They are charged with a higher mission than when they trod the earth. And this thought of the enlargement of their love should enlarge ours, and carry us beyond selfish regards to a benevolence akin to that with which they are inspired.

It is objected, I know, to the view I have given of the connection of the inhabitants of heaven with this world, that it is inconsistent with their happiness. It is said that if they retain their knowledge of this state, they must suffer from the recollection or sight of our sins and woes; that to enjoy heaven, they must wean themselves from the earth. This objection is worse than superficial. It is a reproach to heaven and the good. It supposes that the happiness of that world is founded in ignorance, that it is the happiness of the blind man, who, were he to open his eye on what exists around him, would be filled with horror. It makes heaven an Elysium, whose inhabitants perpetuate their joy by shutting themselves up in narrow bounds, and hiding themselves from the pains of their fellow-creatures. But the good, from their very nature, cannot thus be confined. Heaven would be a prison, did it cut them off from sympathy with the suffering. Their benevolence is too pure, too divine, to shrink from the sight of evil. Let me add, that the objection before us casts reproach on God. It supposes that there are regions of his universe which must be kept out of sight, which, if seen, would blight the happiness of the virtuous. But this cannot be true. There are no such regions, no secret places of woe which these pure spirits must not penetrate. There is impiety in the thought. In such a universe there could be no heaven.

Do you tell me that according to these views suffering must exist in that blessed state? I reply, I do and must regard heaven as a world of sympathy. Nothing, I believe, has greater power to attract the regards of its benevolent inhabitants, than the misery into which any of their fellow-creatures may have fallen. The suffering which belongs to a virtuous sympathy I cannot then separate from heaven. But that sympathy, though it has sorrow, is far from being misery. Even in this world a disinterested compassion, when joined with power to minister to suffering, and with wisdom to comprehend its gracious purposes, is a spirit of peace, and often issues in the purest delight. Unalloyed as it will be in another world by our present infirmities, and enlightened by comprehensive views of God's perfect government, it will give a charm and loveliness to the sublimer virtues of the blessed, and, like all other forms of excellence, will at length enhance their felicity.

We see how much of heaven is taught us in the single truth, that they who enter it meet and are united to Jesus Christ. There are other interesting views at which I can only glance. The departed go not to Jesus only. They go to the great and blessed society which is gathered round him, to the redeemed from all regions of earth, "to the city of the living God, to an innumerable company of angels, to the church of the first born, to the spirits of the just made perfect." Into what a glorious community do they enter! And how they are received you can easily understand. We are told, there is joy in heaven over the sinner who repenteth; and will not his ascension to the abode of perfect virtue communicate more fervent happiness? Our friends who leave us for that world do not find themselves cast among strangers. No desolate feeling springs up of having exchanged their home for a foreign country. The tenderest accents of human friendship never approached in affectionateness the voice of congratulation, which bids them welcome to their new and everlasting abode. In that world, where minds have surer means of revealing themselves than here, the newly arrived immediately see and feel themselves encompassed with virtue and goodness; and through this insight into the congenial spirits which surround them, intimacies stronger than years can cement on earth may be created in a moment.

It seems to me accordant with all the principles of human nature, to suppose that the departed meet peculiar congratulation from friends who had gone before them to that better world; and especially from all who had in any way given aids to their virtue; from parents who had instilled into them the first lessons of love to God and man; from associates, whose examples had won them to goodness, whose faithful counsels deterred them from sin. The ties created by such benefits must be eternal. The grateful soul must bind itself with peculiar affection to such as guided it to immortality.

In regard to the happiness of the intercourse of the future state, all of you, I trust, can form some apprehensions of it. If we have ever known the enjoyments of friendship, of entire confidence, of co-operation in honorable and successful labors with those we love, we can comprehend something of the felicity of a world, where souls, refined from selfishness, open as the day, thirsting for new truth and virtue, endued with new power of enjoying the beauty and grandeur of the universe, allied in the noblest works of benevolence, and continually discovering new mysteries of the Creator's power and goodness, communicate themselves to one another with the freedom of perfect love.

The closest attachments of this life are cold, distant, stranger-like, compared with theirs. How they communicate themselves, by what language or organs, we know not. But this we know, that in the progress of the mind, its power of imparting itself must improve. The eloquence, the thrilling, inspiring tones, in which the good and noble sometimes speak to us on earth, may help us to conceive the expressiveness, harmony, energy of the language in which superior beings reveal themselves above. Of what they converse we can better judge. They who enter that world meet beings whose recollections extend through ages, who have met together perhaps from various worlds, who have been educated amidst infinite varieties of condition, each of whom has passed through his own discipline and reached his own peculiar form of perfection, and each of whom is a peculiar testimony to the providence of the Universal Father. What treasures of memory, observation, experience, imagery, illustration, must enrich the intercourse of heaven! One angel's history may be a volume of more various truth than all the records of our race.—After all, how little can our present experience help us to understand the intercourse of heaven, a communion marred by no passion, chilled by no reserve, depressed by no consciousness of sin, trustful as childhood, and overflowing with innocent joy; a communion in which the noblest feelings spring fresh from the heart, in which pure beings give familiar utterance to their divinest inspirations, to the wonder which perpetually springs up amidst this ever unfolding and ever mysterious universe, to the raptures of adoration and pious gratitude, and to the swellings of a sympathy which cannot be confined.

But it would be wrong to imagine that the inhabitants of heaven only converse. They who reach that world enter on a state of action, life, effort. We are apt to think of the future world as so happy that none need the aid of others, that effort ceases, that the good have nothing to do but to enjoy. The truth is, that all action on earth, even the intensest, is but the sport of childhood, compared with the energy and activity of that higher life. It must be so. For what principles are so active as intellect, benevolence, the love of truth, the thirst for perfection, sympathy with the suffering, and devotion to God's purposes; and these are the ever expanding principles of the future life. It is true, the labors which are now laid on us for food, raiment, outward interests, cease at the grave. But far deeper wants than those of the body are developed in heaven. There it is that the spirit first becomes truly conscious of its capacities; that truth opens before us in its infinity; that the universe is seen to be a boundless sphere for discovery, for science, for the sense of beauty, for beneficence, and for adoration. There new objects to live for, which reduce to nothingness present interests, are constantly unfolded. We must not think of heaven as a stationary community. I think of it as a world of stupendous plans and efforts for its own improvement. I think of it as a society passing through successive stages of development, virtue, knowledge, power, by the energy of its own members. Celestial genius is always active to explore the great laws of the creation and the everlasting principles of the mind, to disclose the beautiful in the universe, and to discover the means by which every soul may be carried forward. In that world, as in this, there are diversities of intellect, and the highest minds find their happiness and progress in elevating the less improved. There the work of education, which began here, goes on without end; and a diviner philosophy than is taught on earth reveals the spirit to itself, and awakens it to earnest, joyful effort for its own perfection.

And not only will they who are born into heaven enter a society full of life and action for its own development. Heaven has connection with other worlds. Its inhabitants are God's messengers through the creation. They have great trusts. In the progress of their endless being they may have the care of other worlds. But I pause, lest to those unused to such speculations I seem to exceed the bounds of calm anticipation. What I have spoken seems to me to rest on God's word, and the laws of the mind, and these laws are everlasting.

On one more topic I meant to enlarge, but I must forbear. They who are born into heaven go, not only to Jesus, and an innumerable company of pure beings. They go to God. They see Him with a new light in all his works. Still more, they see Him, as the Scriptures teach, face to face, that is, by immediate communion. These new relations of the ascended spirit to the Universal Father, how near! how tender! how strong! how exalting! But this is too great a subject for the time which remains. And yet it is the chief element of the felicity of heaven.

The views now given of the future state should make it an object of deep interest, earnest hope, constant pursuit. Heaven is, in truth, a glorious reality. Its attraction should be felt perpetually. It should overcome the force with which this world draws us to itself. Were there a country on earth uniting all that is beautiful in nature, all that is great in virtue, genius, and the liberal arts, and numbering among its citizens the most illustrious patriots, poets, philosophers, philanthropists of our age, how eagerly should we cross the ocean to visit it! And how immeasurably greater is the attraction of heaven! There live the elder brethren of the creation, the sons of the morning, who sang for joy at the creation of our race; there the great and good of all ages and climes; the friends, benefactors, deliverers, ornaments of their race; the patriarch, prophet, apostle, and martyr; the true heroes of public and still more of private life; the father, mother, wife, husband, child, who, unrecorded by man, have walked before God in the beauty of love and self-sacrificing virtue. There are all who have built up in our hearts the power of goodness and truth, the writers from whose pages we have received the inspiration of pure and lofty sentiments, the friends whose countenances have shed light through our dwellings, and peace and strength through our hearts. There they are gathered together, safe from every storm, triumphant over evil; and they say to us, Come and join us in our everlasting blessedness; come and bear part in our song of praise; share our adoration, friendship, progress, and works of love. They say to us, Cherish now in your earthly life that spirit and virtue of Christ which is the beginning and dawn of heaven, and we shall soon welcome you, with more than human friendship, to our own immortality. Shall that voice speak to us in vain? Shall our worldliness and unforsaken sins separate us, by a gulf which cannot be passed, from the society of heaven?

FRIENDS IN HEAVEN.

SEALED is the voice that used to speak
  So gladly of our loved and lost;
And at their names pale is the cheek,
  Even of the friends that loved them most.

A solemn silence shrines the dead—
  A sacred hush—a faltering tone;
And trembling footsteps slowly tread
  Upon the spot so late their own.

Not thus *I* feel their hourly loss—
  I think of them in light and love;
Emblem of life, I view the cross,
  And faith's fond gaze I turn above.

I miss them—ah! in every place;
  I sometimes feel the unbidden tear;
I cherish every fading trace,
  But never, never wish them here.

Their tears are past, their crown is won,
  Th' immortal wreath is all their own;
I seem to hear the chant begun,
  Of joy around th' eternal throne.

Yes, thoughts of peace and holiness
  Surround their images; to me,
'T is not a feeling of distress
  To muse on their loved memory.

'T is hope, 't is triumph, and 't is praise;
  O God! to thee be glory given,
Who, in the darkest of our days,
  Hast linked us to the bliss of heaven.

I will not yield this pure delight
  To vain regrets or faithless sighs;
Memory to me shall shine, a light
  To blend our severed destinies.

HOPE.

O NEVER, never close thy heart
  To human hope—her rapturous power
Shall chase the tear-drops as they start,
  And light with smiles the future hour.

Hope on—hope on—it may not be—
  Yet let thy heart-dreams still be bright;
Still picture that sweet destiny
  In which thy spirit may delight.

Thy friend is at thy side—ah no!
  That friend must find an early tomb,
And death's dark veil conceal below
  That eye of love, that cheek of bloom.

But dearer hopes shall still be thine;
That tender gaze, that angel face
Shall all thy soul's fond hopes enshrine,
And every lighter grief efface.

Alas! that gaze shall coldly change,
That angel glance be thine no more;
And coming years that love estrange,
Which was to bless till life was o'er.

Yet still hope on—though friendship weep,
Thy friend awaits thee 'mongst the blest;
Thy hope, thy faith, thy fondness keep,
Go—seek her in the realms of rest!

Live as she lived—on others pour
The stream of kindness and of peace;
And with deep trust behold the hour
When earth's bereaved tears shall cease.

And for thy lost and broken love,
O! whisper to thy aching heart,
That *He* that anguish can remove,
Whose will supreme first bade you part.

Yes! thou shalt meet that angel gaze,
Again thine own, in realms of bliss,
Where love shall wear immortal rays,
And, unreproved, thy heart be his.

Hope on—hope on—for joy is here,
Even in this dark and chequered scene;
Go! chase thy every doubt and tear,
Thy life a *Father's* care hath been.

THANKSGIVING IN AFFLICTION.

In times of trouble prayer to God is as natural as it is right; but who can sing the songs of praise under the clouds of sorrow, and amidst the waters of affliction? What connection is there between thanksgiving and distress?

We may observe, in general, that afflictions are not evils. Let me not be mistaken; I mean not to deny that nature shrinks from them; I mean not to insinuate, that we can by any means render ourselves insensible to pain and sorrow. I speak not of the present pressure of affliction, but with respect to the future consequences of present suffering; with respect to the moral influences of adversity; with respect to the fair and the abundant fruits of holiness and happiness, which, by faith and patience and diligence, it may be made to yield. I speak with regard to the *whole*, both of our condition and our existence; and when it is asserted that afflictions are not evils, it is meant, that without them we should have less comfort in this present scene of things, or fewer advantages in our power with respect to that eternal state which is soon to succeed it. They do, or at least, if it is not our own fault, they may advance our interests upon the whole, and therefore are not upon the whole evils.

No evil being has any thing to do in the government of the world; it is ruled by the God of love. Our sharpest pains, our severest anguish, are not the cruelties of a malignant principle, they are not the barbarous sport of an insensible and wanton mind; they are not blown to us by the wind of chance, nor borne down upon us by the torrent of an unintelligent and irresistible destiny. They are the gracious visitations of our heavenly Father, without whom not a sparrow falleth to the ground, nor a hair from the human head. We call them evils, and yet they come from the pure and incorruptible fountain of all good; and it is with the kindest intention that they are sent to us. Did we see with the eyes of God, we should call them all blessings; for they are all alike capable of being converted by us to our interest, and all alike intended to do us good. If any confidence can be placed in the clearest deductions of reason, this is an indubitable consequence of the absolute independence and infinite perfection of God. The word of God is as clear and full as we could wish it, on a point of such mighty moment to our tranquillity and comfort. How often are we told there, that nothing happens to us but by his appointment; that there is no evil, nothing that we blindly call so, but of his creating; that he has no pleasure either in the destruction or the distresses of his creatures; that he does not willingly afflict or grieve the children of men; that he chastens them, not for his own pleasure but for their profit, that they may be made "partakers of his holiness." How often are we taught that the sufferings of life are not the tokens of divine wrath, but the testimonies of God's paternal attention and compassion; that the trials of adversity, the various calamities with which we are visited, are calculated to promote our virtue, to improve our comfort, to secure our best interest, and to enlarge our heavenly inheritance. The light affliction of this transitory world, "which is but for a moment, worketh out for us a far more exceeding and eternal weight of glory."

If such then be the nature of afflictions; if such be the principle from which they come; if such be their genuine tendency, and such the advantages they put into our hands, have we no reason to give thanks for them? Difficult it may be, but unreasonable it is not.

No man can be at a loss to say, which hath tho greater obligation to his father, the child that is suffered, without discipline or culture, to grow up in ignorance and folly, the slave of humor, appetite and passion; or the child whose prejudices are carefully corrected, whose follies are properly rebuked, whose faults are mercifully and calmly, yet steadily and uniformly chastised, and who is instructed, or assisted to instruct himself, in whatever is of most importance to the interests of his future life; and it is not to be doubted, that when they have each attained to maturity of judgment, and acquired experience in human things, the one will lament the blind indulgence that permitted him without interruption to enjoy himself according to his own will, and the other will rejoice in the hardships to which he was inured, and will estimate even the severities, that excited no gratitude at the time, among the truest arguments of parental tenderness and love. This whole life, in respect to the whole of our existence, is a scene of discipline and education; have we not reason to rejoice in the superintendence of our heavenly Father? If we were left without the instructions and admonitions, without the correctives and corroborations of adversity, then would he not deal with us as sons.

But, to put the discipline of this life as it affects the interests of the next out of the account—to consider only the enjoyment of our present being; it might bear a doubt, whether such sufferings as ordinarily fall to the lot of men, together with the supports, the consolations, the deliverances that are ordinarily granted them, do not make, or put it in our power to make, even this present state a more desirable and more comfortable scene, than if every species of adversity were absolutely excluded from it. There is a joy in deliverance, that exists not in uninterrupted security; there is a delight in the restoration of a comfort, which for a time has been either totally or in part suspended, that is not to be found in the continued possession of it. There are a multitude of soothing satisfactions that are peculiar to the hour of trouble. While we reflect on the blessings that remain, they are the more endeared to us; when we experience the efficacy of those supports with which God has furnished us, how sweet are our reflections on the tenderness of our heavenly Father, who never leaves us nor forsakes us; who forgetteth not how frail we are; and who in the midst of judgment remembers mercy!

What joy is it to the Christian, (and all men may attain the Christian temper,) what joy is it to reflect that his trials have not overcome his faith, nor extinguished his devotion, nor diminished his alacrity in the service of his Maker? What joy is it that he bears, or strives to bear, his burdens with a decent composure, and that he improves, or labors to improve them with all fidelity and diligence? Into what tenderness does not sorrow melt the heart of friendship? What unusual and delightful acceptableness does it not impart to all its services? What stability and firmness does it not forever add unto the union?

These things, if we attend to them, may suffice to satisfy us, that with respect even to the enjoyment of the present life, it is no undesirable thing that we should sometimes receive the visits of adversity.

I will not ask the sinner if he has no cause to be thankful for the afflictions that recall him from his wanderings, and cure him of his levity, and bring him back to God. Let me ask the Christian, who may perhaps think that he stands less in need of such distasteful dispensations, if there be no cause for thankfulness in circumstances that may enliven his conviction of his own weakness and insufficiency, and of his absolute dependence upon God? in circumstances that most feelingly demonstrate to him the importance of the divine favor, and the vanity of all human things? in circumstances that most powerfully incline him to serious thought and sincere devotion; that melt his heart into all the sweet and amiable sympathies of

Christian charity and love; that clothe him more gracefully than ever in humility; that engage him in the most accurate examination of his heart and conduct, and that quicken the sentiments of patience, and strengthen his resolutions of obedience? In such circumstances, Christian, is there nothing for which thou shouldst give thanks? These advantages affliction offers thee; these uses thou mayst make of it. Whilst thou prayest to God, then, that he would give thee grace so to improve them, shouldst thou not give thanks that thou hast them in thy hands so to be improved?

In our afflictions it becomes us to unite thanksgivings with our prayers for another reason also, viz. that our sufferings are not so great as our demerit. What, may the Christian say, had been my condition, if it had been determined by my merit? If for every instance in which I had forgotten God he had forgotten me and my concerns, if for every duty I had neglected he had subtracted but one from my comforts and enjoyments, if for every deviation I have made from the way of his commandments his chastisements had come upon me; my hopes would have been extinguished, my comforts have been exhausted, and my miseries have been already insupportable. "How precious are his thoughts unto me! how great is the sum of them!" It is true, I have been happier; but while I can hope in God that he will extend his compassion to me, and can rejoice in his benignity that he has not chastened me according to my demerit, but according to his own goodness, I am not unhappy still. Thy mercy, O my God, appears in every dispensation of thy providence. The prosperities thou bestowest on me demand my gratitude, for I am not worthy of them; I am not even worthy to be chastened with so much tenderness and pity.

Such, in regard to the dispensations of Divine Providence, are the sentiments of every heart that is truly Christian. In this manner does the Christian own his obligation in all things to give thanks.

In the hour of trouble it likewise becomes us to offer thanks because, let our condition be what it may, it is not so afflictive as it might have been.

In every sorrow that you have ever yet experienced, it would be very easy for you to imagine what would have greatly aggravated and embittered it. There were still some powers of your nature, there were still some circumstances of your situation, which the arrows of adversity had not reached. If you were poor, perhaps you were in health; if you were sick, perhaps you did not want what might procure you wherewith to mitigate and remove your sicknesses. If your bodies were diseased, your minds were not disordered, you were still possessed of your rational and moral powers; and though your bodily diseases were many, you were not exercised with all the pains and sicknesses that might have been combined together; it is probable you might have recollected among your friends, perhaps you might have found within your neighborhood, those that were at that very time proved with more. If your friends were in trouble, yet it was only some, not all of them; you perhaps were not afflicted but in their affliction: if *you* were in trouble, *they* perhaps were not afflicted but in yours. You were not incapacitated for performing the offices of friendship for them, nor they withheld from rendering the like services to you.

If your troubles were of such a nature as to admit of human consolation and relief, it is probable that they befell you in a scene, and at a time, when such aids and comforts might be obtained. If of such a nature they were not, and the whole burden must have been borne by yourself alone, it is very probable you can call to remembrance those seasons and conjunctures of your life, those states of mind, of body, or of circumstances which formerly you have experienced, in which it was possible you might have been placed again, wherein the troubles that oppressed you would have borne upon you much more heavily, and have affected you with much keener and more insupportable distress.

If your anguish has been very sharp, it has not been very tedious; if your sorrow has been of some continuance, it has not been without intervals of comfort and enjoyment, and perhaps all along it has been very tolerable. If the afflictions which you have feared have overtaken you, yet you feared them perhaps some time before you felt them, and when they came, though you found them very painful, yet not so distressing as you feared. They might have embittered life much sooner, they might have embittered it much more.

In every scene of affliction, in every hour of trouble, there is something for which we may, something for which, if we would be faithful to our duty, we must give thanks. There is no condition of human life that we ever have experienced, or ever shall, from which some consolations, still left us, might not have been withdrawn; to which some sorrow might not have been added; in which some circumstances might not have been altered for the worse.

It becomes us also, in our afflictions, to unite thanksgiving with our supplication, because our afflictions in this life never are so great but that they admit of consolation.

Diseases both of body and mind are in very many instances capable of being cured by proper applications; and even in those instances where they prove incurable, the anguish of them, ordinarily at least, is capable of being mitigated; and such is the benignity of God, that both in the material and spiritual worlds he hath furnished us with a variety of remedies and lenitives for the various pains and distresses to which we are liable. It is a law of our nature that reflects the greatest honor on the Author of it, and calls upon us for perpetual gratitude, that in many cases, the longer we suffer, the lighter our sufferings become. If our pleasures please us less when they are become habitual, this is abundantly made up to us in the counterpart of the appointment—that our distresses distress us less, as we become inured to them.

Prayer is another of the comforts of which we may avail ourselves in our afflictions; it is a comfort which God extends to us, and which he means, which he expects, which he requires us to take. To our dutiful endeavors to sustain our sorrows, we may add our pious supplications for support and comfort and relief; and having done this, we cannot in any circumstances, however distressing, be devoid of hope. Hope is the great cordial of human life. It must mingle with our most prosperous circumstances, or the enjoyment of them will be but very dull and languid and imperfect: without hope, the adversities of life, even in the lightest instances, would sit heavily on our hearts; and on the contrary, our most grievous sufferings yield in some measure to its cheering influences. In our worst condition, we are not without hope that the day is coming when it may be better with us; our pains may cease, our fears may vanish; our difficulties may find a period at last; by and by our tears may be dried up, and our wounded hearts be healed. If no other hope remain to us, yet we know that ere long we shall arrive at those peaceful mansions where the weary are at rest. Our troubles will at least cease there. Death will compose our fears and take away our pains. Though no bright interval should gild the remainder of the day, when once the sun of life is set, the night we know will be still and easy; we shall rest then, if not before; and if our state be such that we find no intermission of our anguish, that night is probably not far off.

These hopes nothing can take from us: we have no pains that are immortal. The storms of life must drive us to the haven whither we are steering. Let us keep our good character, and we cannot miss our port. When sorrows press upon us, it is a sweet reflection, a thought that soothes the anguish of our hearts, that by and by we shall shut our eyes on all that troubles us, and lay ourselves down, to be disturbed no more. But how much sweeter, how much more soothing is the thought, of what mighty power, Christian, have you not often found it to cheer you in a dark and painful hour, that when we are retired from this world's troubles, we shall be received to that where no tribulations come; to pure, and endless and inconceivable felicity. This hope is indeed an anchor of the soul, sure and steadfast; the consolation it contains is unspeakable. The vale of death is peaceful, the world to which it leads is glorious and happy. Happy man whose inheritance is there! Why will not all men be so happy? Happy he whose hope can anticipate his arrival there! He is well prepared for all the calamities of life; he can never want a cordial to support him under them; he has reason, and will ordinarily have the disposition too, to rejoice evermore. He cannot guard himself, and he knows that God neither should nor will defend him from the common calamities of life; but whatever may happen, nothing can come without his own consent, that shall destroy his eternal interests. These consolations, some of them we *must* have, all of them we *may* have, in every hour of trouble, and through every hour of life. Say, then, is the advice impracticable, is the command unreasonable, that in our afflictions we should give thanks? Much matter for thanksgiving we can never fail to have.

Our prayers and supplications in the day of our adversity ought further to be accompanied with thanksgiving, because present troubles do not annihilate former mercies.

If you have lost a blessing, you have had one; it may be that you have had it long; it may be that the time you have been happy in the possession of it is much longer than the time for which you will be afflicted by its loss. It is now taken from you, but the value of the blessing is not hereby diminished; the period during which you were indulged by it is not hereby shortened; the enjoyment was as real as the loss.

Has sickness seized you? There is room for thankfulness that you know the difference between a state of sickness and a state of health. Have you lost a friend? You had a friend to lose. Have you lost, unjustly lost, your esteem and credit in the world? It is true, notwithstanding, that for a time you enjoyed the good opinion of the world, and your obligations unto God who gave you to enjoy it for that period are in this respect unaltered and unalterable. You cannot, it is true, thank God for a blessing he has taken from you; but it is your duty, even when it is not permitted you to retain it, it is still your duty to give thanks to him that you had that blessing once, and that it was not taken from you sooner. There was a portion of your life that was happier than it would have been without it;

ought you not then to bless him for the past, while you implore his pity on the present? Does it not become you, while you beseech him to comfort you under the loss, to thank him that he blessed you with the enjoyment? I said, but perhaps I ought not to have said, that you cannot thank God for a blessing which he has taken from you; for methinks, if reason have that authority which she ought to have over your affections, you will be able, even after you have lost the comforts in which you delighted most, in some measure to re-enjoy the pleasures that they gave you. Though the blessing be gone, your memory is not gone with it; and whilst this remains, you may avail yourself of its aid to supply the absence of the comfort you have lost, by bringing back into the present the enjoyments of the past. To a mind that is properly affected, it gives less pain than pleasure in sickness to recollect the season of health; in poverty, the time of affluence; in separation from friends, the period of communion with them; in adversity, of whatever kind, the day of prosperity. Thus we may in a manner perpetuate enjoyments, and with them our gratitude; the pleasure may not be so pure and lively, but it is by no means unreal. Our blessings may administer to our comfort even after we are deprived of them; the present may be made more happy by the remembrance of the past. The perverseness of mankind, it is true, very often employs their recollection to increase their misery. They may use it for a better purpose; and is not this a state of mind, after which it is desirable for ourselves and dutiful towards God, that we should carefully aspire? But,

We may add, finally, that our comforts, though dead, are in very many instances not absolutely lost to us: they still live in their influences and their consequences. All our past enjoyments, though the immediate instruments or sources of them be no more, have each had their efficacy in the great chain of Providence, have each contributed their share to form the present conjuncture of our circumstances, and to give their present aspect to our affairs. Affluent if you have been, you have derived some benefits from that affluence that remain with you in your poverty; and if any man has had a kind, a wise and pious friend, though it may not be in his power perhaps to specify them, he must have derived some benefits from that friendship, that will live with him long after that friend is dead; and it may be, long after he is dead himself. The same might be said of many other blessings once enjoyed and then lost again. Ought we not then, though we have lost them, to give thanks?

So good was the Apostle's counsel, so wise are they that keep it,—"In all things, therefore, by prayer and supplication, with thanksgiving let your requests be made known unto God."

TRUST AMIDST TRIAL.

FATHER! I thank thee; may no thought
  E'er deem thy chastisements severe;
But may this heart, by sorrow taught,
  Calm each wild wish, each idle fear.

Thy mercy bids all nature bloom:
  The sun shines bright, and man is gay·
Thine equal mercy spreads the gloom,
  That darkens o'er his little day.

Full many a throb of grief and pain
  Thy frail and erring child must know
But not one prayer is breathed in vain,
  Nor does one tear unheeded flow.

Thy various messengers employ;
  Thy purposes of love fulfil;
And 'mid the wreck of human joy
  May kneeling faith adore thy will.

LIFE AND DEATH.

  OH fear not thou to die!
But rather fear to live; for Life
Has thousand snares thy feet to try
  By peril, pain, and strife.

Brief is the work of Death;
But Life! the spirit shrinks to see
How full, ere Heaven recalls the breath,
The cup of woe may be.

Oh fear not thou to die!
No more to suffer or to sin;
No snares without thy faith to try,
No traitor heart within;
But fear, oh! rather fear
The gay, the light, the changeful scene,
The flattering smiles that greet thee here,
From Heaven thy heart that wean.

Fear lest in evil hour,
Thy pure and holy hope o'ercome
By clouds that in the horizon lower,
Thy spirit feel that gloom,
Which over earth and heaven
The covering throws of fell despair,
And deem itself the unforgiven,
Predestined child of care.

Oh fear not thou to die!
To die, and be that blessed one,
Who, in the bright and beauteous sky,
May feel his conflict done;
Who feels that never more
The tear of grief or shame shall come,
For thousand wanderings from that Power,
Who loved, and called him home.

THE VOICES OF THE DEAD.

The world is filled with the voices of the dead. They speak not from the public records of the great world only, but from the private history of our own experience. They speak to us in a thousand remembrances, in a thousand incidents, events, associations. They speak to us, not only from their silent graves, but from the throng of life. Though they are invisible, yet life is filled with their presence. They are with us by the silent fireside and in the secluded chamber; they are with us in the paths of society, and in the crowded assembly of men. They speak to us from the lonely way-side; and they speak to us from the venerable walls that echo to the steps of a multitude, and to the voice of prayer. Go where we will, the dead are with us. We live, we converse, with those who once lived and conversed with us. Their well remembered tone mingles with the whispering breezes, with the sound of the falling leaf, with the jubilee shout of the spring-time. The earth is filled with their shadowy train. Let us look upon ourselves in this relation, and see what we owe to the dead.

What memories, then, have the dead left among us, to stimulate us to virtue, to win us to goodness.

The approach to death often prepares the way for this impression. The effect of a last sickness to develop and perfect the virtues of our friends, is often so striking and beautiful, as to seem more than a compensation for all the sufferings of disease. It is the practice of the Catholic church to bestow upon its eminent saints a title to the perpetual homage of the faithful, in the act of canonization But what is a formal decree, compared with the effect of a last sickness, to canonize the virtue that we love, for eternal

12

remembrance and admiration? How often does that touching decay, that gradual unclothing of the mortal body, seem to be a putting on of the garments of immortal beauty and life! That pale cheek, that placid brow, that sweet serenity spread over the whole countenance, that spiritual, almost supernatural brightness of the eye, as if light from another world already shone through it, that noble and touching disinterestedness of the parting spirit, which utters no complaint, which breathes no sigh, which speaks no word of fear nor apprehension to wound its friend—which is calm, and cheerful, and natural, and self-sustained, amidst daily declining strength and the sure approach to death—and then, at length, when concealment is no longer possible, that last firm, triumphant, consoling discourse, and that last look of all mortal tenderness and immortal trust;—what hallowed memories are these to soothe, to purify, to enrapture surviving love!

Death, too, sets a seal upon the excellence that sickness unfolds and consecrates. There is no living virtue concerning which—such is our frailty—we must not fear that it may fall; or, at least, that it may somewhat fail from its steadfastness. It is a painful, it is a just fear, in the bosoms of the best and purest beings on earth, that some dreadful lapse *may* come over them, or over those whom they hold in the highest reverence. But death, fearful, mighty as its power, is yet a power that is subject to virtue. It gives victory to virtue. It brings relief to the heart from its profoundest fear. It enables us to say, "Now all is safe! The battle is fought; the victory is won. The course is finished; the race is run; the faith is kept: henceforth, it is no more doubt nor danger, no more temptation nor strife; henceforth is the reward of the just, the crown which the Lord, the righteous Judge, will give!" Yes, death—dark power of earth though it seem—does yet ensphere virtue, as it were, in heaven. It sets it up on high, for eternal admiration. It fixes its place never more to be changed—as a star to shine onward, and onward, through the depths of the everlasting ages!

In life there are many things which interfere with a just estimate of the virtues of others. There are, in some cases, jealousies, and misconstructions, and there are false appearances; there are veils upon the heart that hide its most secret workings and its sweetest affections from us; there are earthly clouds that come between us and the excellence that we love. So that it is not, perhaps, till a friend is taken from us, that we entirely feel his value, and appreciate his worth. The vision is loveliest at its vanishing away; and we perceive not, perhaps, till we see the parting wing, that an angel has been with us.

Yet if we are not, from any cause, or in any degree, blind to the excellence we possess, if we do feel all the value of the treasure which our affections hold dear; yet, I say, how does that earthly excellence take not only a permanent, but a saintly character, as it passes beyond the bounds of mortal frailty and imperfection! how does death enshrine it, for a homage, more reverential and holy than is ever given to living worth! So that the virtues of the dead gain, perhaps, in the power of sanctity, what they lose in the power of visible presence; and thus—it may not be too much to say—thus the virtues of the dead benefit us sometimes as much as the examples of living goodness.

How beautiful is the ministration by which those who are dead thus speak to us—thus help us, comfort us, guide, gladden, bless us! How grateful must it be to their thoughts of us, to know that we thus remember them; that we remember them, not with mere admiration, but in a manner that ministers to all our virtues! What a glorious vision of the future is it, to the good and pure who are yet living on earth, that the virtues which they are cherishing and manifesting, the good character which they are building up here, the charm of their benevolence and piety, shall live when they have laid down the burthen and toil of life—shall be an inspiring breath to the fainting hearts that are broken from them—a wafted odour of sanctity to hundreds and thousands that shall come after them. Is it not so? Are there not those, the simplest story, the frailest record of whose goodness, is still, and ever, doing good? But frail records, we know full well, frail records they are *not*, which are in our hearts. And can we have known those whom it is a joy, as well as a sorrow, to think of, and not be better for it? Are there those—once our friends, now bright angels, in some blessed sphere—and do we not sometimes say, "Perhaps that pure eye of affection is on me now; and I will do nothing to wound it?" No, surely, it cannot be, that the dead will speak to us in vain. Their memories are all around us: their footsteps are in our paths; the memorials of them meet our eye at every turn; their presence is in our dwellings; their voices are in our ears; they speak to us—in the sad reverie of contemplation, in the sharp pang of feeling, in the cold shadow of memory, in the bright light of hope—and it cannot be that they will speak in vain.

The dead not only leave their own enshrined and canonized virtues for us to love and imitate; but they open a future world to our vision, and invite us to its blessed abodes.

They open that world to us by giving, in their own deaths, a strong proof of its existence.

The future, indeed, to mere earthly views, is often "a land of darkness as darkness itself, and of the shadow of death without any order, and where the light is as darkness." Truly, death is "without any order." There is in it such a total disregard to circumstances, as shows that it cannot be an ultimate event. That must be connected with something else; that cannot be final, which, considered as final, puts all the calculations of wisdom so utterly at defiance. The tribes of animals, the classes and species of the vegetable creation, come to their perfection, and then die. But is there any such order for human beings? Do the generations of mankind go down to the grave in ranks and processions? Are the human, like the vegetable races, suffered to stand till they have made provision for their successors, before they depart? No; without order, without discrimination, without provision for the future or remedy for the past, the children of men depart. They die—the old, the young; the most useless, and those most needed; the worst and the best alike die; and if there be no scenes beyond this life, if there be no circumstances nor allotments to explain the mystery, then all around us is, as it was to the doubting spirit of Job, "a land of darkness as darkness itself." The blow falls, like the thunderbolt beneath the dark cloud; but it has not even the intention, the explanation, that belongs to that dread minister. The stroke of death must be more reckless than even the lightning's flash—yes, that solemn visitation that cometh with so many dread signs—the body's dissolution, the spirit's extremity, the winding up of the great scene of life, has not even the meaning that belongs to the blindest agents in nature, if there be no reaction, no revelation hereafter! Can this be? Doth God take care for things animate and inanimate, and will he not care for us?

Let us look at it for a moment. I have seen one die—the delight of his friends, the pride of his kindred, the hope of his country: but he died! How beautiful was that offering upon the altar of death! The fire of genius kindled in his eye; the generous affections of youth mantled in his cheek; his foot was upon the threshold of life; his studies, his preparations for honored and useful life, were completed; his breast was filled with a thousand glowing, and noble, and never yet expressed aspirations: but he died! He died! while another, of a nature dull, coarse, and unrefined, of habits low, base, and brutish, of a promise that had nothing in it but shame and misery—such an one, I say, was suffered to encumber the earth. Could this be, if there were no other sphere for the gifted, the aspiring, and the approved, to act in? Can we believe that the energy just trained for action, the embryo thought just bursting into expression, the deep and earnest passion of a noble nature, just swelling into the expansion of every beautiful virtue, should never manifest its power, should never speak, should never unfold itself? Can we believe that all this should die; while meanness, corruption, sensuality, and every deformed and dishonored power, should live? No, ye goodly and glorious ones! ye godlike in youthful virtue! ye die not in vain; ye teach, ye assure us, that ye are gone to some world of nobler life and action.

I have seen one die; she was beautiful; and beautiful were the ministries of life that were given her to fulfil. Angelic loveliness enrobed her; and a grace as if it were caught from heaven breathed in every tone, hallowed every affection, shone in every action—invested, as a halo, her whole existence, and made it a light and blessing, a charm and a vision of gladness, to all around her: but she died! Friendship, and love, and parental fondness, and infant weakness, stretched out their hand to save her; but they could not save her; and she died! What! did all that loveliness die? Is there no land of the blessed and the lovely ones, for such to live in? Forbid it, reason, religion!—bereaved affection, and undying love! forbid the thought! It cannot be that such die in God's counsel, who live even in frail human memory forever!

I have seen one die—in the maturity of every power, in the earthly perfection of every faculty; when many temptations had been overcome, and many hard lessons had been learned; when many experiments had made virtue easy, and had given a facility to action, and a success to endeavor; when wisdom had been learned from many mistakes, and a skill had been laboriously acquired in the use of many powers; and the being I looked upon had just compassed that most useful, most practical of all knowledge, how to live, and to act well and wisely; yet I have seen such an one die! Was all this treasure gained only to be lost? Were all these faculties trained only to be thrown into utter disuse? Was this instrument—the intelligent soul, the noblest in the universe—was it so laboriously fashioned, and by the most varied and expensive apparatus, that, on the very moment of being finished, it should be cast away forever? No, the dead, as we call them, do not *so* die. They carry our thoughts to another and a nobler existence. They teach us, and especially by all the strange and seemingly untoward circumstances of their departure from this life, that they, and we, shall live forever. They open the future world, then, to our faith.

They open it also, and in fine, to our affections. No person of reflection and piety can have lived long without beginning to find, in regard to the earthly objects that most interest him,—his friends—that the balance is gradually inclining in favor of another world. How many, after the middle period of life, and especially in declining years, must feel—if the experience of life has had any just effect upon them—that the objects of their strongest attachment are not here. One by one, the ties of earthly affection are cut asunder; one by one, friends, companions, children, parents, are taken from us; for a time, perhaps, we are "in a strait betwixt two," as was the apostle, not deciding altogether whether it is better to depart; but shall we not, at length, say with the disciples, when some dearer friend is taken, "let us go and die with him?"

The dead have not ceased their communication with us, though the visible chain is broken. If they are still the same, they must still think of us. As two friends on earth may know that they love each other without any expression, without even the sight of each other; as they may know, though dwelling in different and distant countries, without any visible chain of communication, that their thoughts meet and mingle together; so may it be with two friends of whom the one is on earth and the other is in heaven. Especially where there is such a union of pure minds that it is scarcely possible to conceive of separation, that union seems to be a part of their very being; we may believe that their friendship, their mutual sympathy, is beyond the power of the grave to break up. "But ah! we say, if there were only some manifestation; if there were only a glimpse of that blessed land; if there were, indeed, some messenger bird, such as is supposed in some countries to come from the spirit land, how eagerly should we question it!" In the words of the poet, we should say,

"But tell us, thou bird of the solemn strain,
Can those who have loved, forget?
We call, but *they* answer not again;
Do they love, do they love us yet?

We call them far, through the silent night,
And they speak not from cave nor hill;
We know, we know, that their land is bright,
But say, do they love there still?"

The poetic doubt we may answer with plain reasoning, and plainer scripture. We may say, in the language of reason, if they *live* there, they love there. We may answer in the language of Jesus Christ, "he that liveth and believeth in me shall never die." And again; "Have ye not read," saith our Savior, "that which was spoken unto you by God, saying, I am the God of Abraham, and the God of Isaac, and the God of Jacob? God is not the God of the dead, but of the living." Then is it true that they live there; and they yet speak to us. From that bright sphere, from that calm region, from the bowers of life immortal, they speak to us. They say to us, "Sigh not in despair over the broken and defeated expectations of earth. Sorrow not as those who have no hope. Bear, calmly and cheerfully, thy lot. Brighten the chain of love, of sympathy, of communion with all pure minds, on earth, and in heaven. Think, oh! think of the mighty and glorious company that fill the immortal regions. Light, life, beauty, beatitude, are here. Come, children of earth! come to the bright and blessed land!" I see no lovely features revealing themselves through the dim and shadowy veils of heaven. I see no angel forms enrobed with the bright clouds of eventide. But "I hear a voice, saying, write, blessed are the dead who die in the Lord, for they rest—for they rest from their labors, and their works—works of piety and love recorded in our hearts and kept in eternal remembrance—their works do follow them." Our hearts—their workmanship—do follow them. We will go and die with them. We will go and live with them forever!

Oh! death!—dark hour to hopeless unbelief! hour to which, in that creed of despair, no hour shall succeed! being's last hour! to whose appalling darkness even the shadows of an avenging retribution were brightness and relief—death! what art thou to the Christian's assurance? Great hour of answer to life's prayer—great hour that shall break asunder the bond of life's mystery—hour of release from life's burden—hour of reunion with the loved and lost—what mighty hopes hasten to their fulfilment in thee! What longings, what aspirations,—breathed in the still night, beneath the silent stars—what dread emotions of curiosity—what deep meditations of joy—what hallowed imaginings of never experienced purity and bliss—what possibilities shadowing forth unspeakable realities to the soul, all verge to their consummation in thee! Oh! death! the Christian's death! what art thou but the gate of life, the portal of heaven, the threshold of eternity!

VOICES OF THE DEAD.

Oh! there are moments when the cares of life
Press on the wearied spirit; when the heart
Is fainting in the conflict, and the crown,
The bright, immortal crown for which we strive,
Shines dimly through the gathering mists of earth.
Then, Voices of the Dead! sweet, solemn Voices!
How have I heard ye, in my inmost soul!
Voices of those who, while they walked on earth,
Were linked unto my spirit by the ties
Of pure affection—love more strong than death!
Ye cry, "Frail child of earth! tried, tempted one!
Shrink not! despond not! strive as we have striven
In the stern conflict; yet a little while,
And thou shalt be as we are; thou shalt know
How far the recompense transcends the toil."

Sweet sister! thou wert parted from my side,
Ere yet one shade had dimmed thy loveliness—
While still the holy light of innocence
Was radiant round thee; thou hast past away,
In purity unsullied, to his bosom,
Who in his love said, "Suffer little children
To come unto me, and forbid them not."
Mine only sister! thou art calling me—
By all a sister's love, by every hope

Which withered at thy tomb to bloom in heaven—
To that bright home, where all the severed links
Of the dear household band again shall join,
Nor through eternity the silver chain
Of purity, and love, and peace, be broken.

Friend of my youth! how lately, in thy beauty
And gladness, thou wert with me! Life's young flowers
Were budding round us;—now, my lips have pressed
Their last, sad kiss upon thy pale, calm brow,
And the delight of many eyes is hid
In the dark house of death. My friend! My friend!
'T is thy sweet voice is pleading—shall the hope
Which tinged, as with a ray of heavenly light,
The clouds which gathered round the parting hour—
The blessed hope of meeting thee again,
Where death is not, be lightly cast away?

My mother! O my mother! thoughts of thee
Come o'er my spirit, like the dews of heaven
Upon the fainting flowers. Best beloved
Of all the dear departed! to thy child
Thine image rises, in thy mournful sweetness
And touching beauty, fading from the earth.
I hear thy voice as when I knelt before thee,
And thou didst lay thy hand upon my head,
And raise thy tearful eyes to heaven in prayer
To Him, who, though the mother leave her child,
Will not forsake the orphan. Thy full soul
Was poured in supplication, dying saint!

Wert thou not heard? surely thou wert! by Him
Who, loving thee, hath called thee to himself!
Surely thou wert!—even now that voice of prayer
Is floating round me, breathing hope and peace.
Thy God has been my God—thy trust, my trust;
His goodness faileth not. O, may he grant,
That yet again the mother with her child
May bow to worship Him, the Merciful,
In that bright temple where no tone of sorrow
Is mingling in the rapturous burst of praise!

TO THE MEMORY OF A FRIEND.

We miss thy voice while early flowers are blowing,
And the first flush of blossom clothes each bough,
And the spring sunshine round our home is glowing
Soft as thy smile—thou shouldst be with us now!

With *us!*—we wrong thee by the earthly thought—
Could our fond gaze but follow where thou art,
Well might the glories of this world seem nought
To the one promise given the pure in heart.

Yet wert thou blest e'en here—oh! ever blest
In thine own sunny thoughts and tranquil faith;
The silent joy that still o'erflowed thy breast,
Needed but guarding from all change, by death.

So is it sealed to peace!—on thy clear brow
Never was care one fleeting shade to cast,
And thy calm days in brightness were to flow,
A holy stream, untroubled to the last!

Farewell! thy life hath left surviving love
  A wealth of records and sweet "feelings given,"
From sorrow's heart the faintness to remove,
  By whispers breathing "less of earth than heaven."

Thus rests thy spirit still on those with whom
  Thy step the paths of joyous duty trod,
Bidding them make an altar of thy tomb,
  Where chastened thought may offer praise to God!

A PRAYER IN AFFLICTION.

Let me not wander comfortless,
  My Father, far from thee,
But still, beneath thy guardian wing.
  In holy quiet be.

The storms of grief, the tears of woe,
  Soothed by thy love, shall cease,
And all the trembling spirit breathe
  A deep, unbroken peace.

The power of prayer shall o'er me shed
  A soft celestial calm;
Sweeter than evening's twilight dews.
  My soul shall drink its balm.

For there the still small voice shall speak
  Thy great, thy boundless love;
And angel forms the mourner call
  To the bright realms above.

DUTIES OF THE AFFLICTED.

THE afflicted are not commonly addressed on the subject of their duties. We find ourselves disposed rather to sympathize with, than to exhort them. Grief is privileged, and we presume not to approach it, except with tenderness and respect. It is already bowed down. If we could, we would relieve it of the burdens which it bears; we would not lay other burdens upon it.

But the thought of duties which it owes is not to a good mind a burdensome thought, nor is the recommendation of them felt by such a mind to be an unkindness. A true sympathy dictates a regard to the best good, the religious good, of the objects of its concern, and, as far as it can excite them to a conduct becoming their condition, it is assured that it will at the same time lighten their grief. The afflicted have their duties,- and these demanding only the more to be considered on account of the allowances which they are tempted to make for themselves, and the indulgence with which any weakness of theirs is naturally regarded by others. To a brief suggestion of some of these let our attention now be given.

The obligation to preserve moderation in sorrow may be first named.

We are not taught that we must not grieve. If it be right to prize the blessings which God gives, it cannot be wrong to be pained when he recalls them. We are not prohibited from a strong grief. Jesus, our master and example, wept. But what is enjoined on us to avoid is, a sorrow such as those indulge who are without hope; that is, a despairing, an abandoned sorrow. Moderation, indeed, is a somewhat indefinite word. Its requisitions vary with different circumstances, so that what is moderation in one case would be excess and extravagance in another. But we sufficiently well understand that immoderate feelings are such as exceed the bounds, which, in the given case, reason and sense of duty, in a fair consideration of their dictates, prescribe; and we shall not in practice be often wrong in deciding where this censure ought to attach. In fact, there will not be presented occasion for nice distinctions in the exercise of that judgment; for the extravagance which will not keep due limits, will, of its nature, go on to overstep them far and manifestly.

We are evidently depressed to an inordinate degree, if we suffer any minor evils to bring an habitual gloom over our spirits, and distrust over our views of life. There are those, it may be feared, to whom any undesirable occurrence, though itself of no considerable moment, is a sort of signal for all painful thoughts to throng into the mind. What they have endured, they permit to color their view of every object. What existed just as much before as now, and was just as real an evil, but one which they either saw to be trifling, or had trained themselves to account tolerable, appears, under the new influence which has been exerted, in quite another aspect. But lately they were contented; but some single cause of dissatisfaction has arisen, and in the altered hue which, instead of contemplating it and disposing of it alone, they have suffered it to give to their spirits, they have proceeded to call up all painful subjects of reflection accessible to their imaginations; and their minds are filled with darkness.

This is a very reprehensible as well as unfortunate habit of mind. Sufficient for the resources as well as the endurance of the day is the evil thereof; and to call up other troubles because there is one with which we must needs contend, is no act of Christian prudence. But our attention is rather due to those on whom has fallen the blow of some real adversity. Their grief, though such as to move human sympathy and divine compassion, they must allow would be blamable if it should be indulged without measure and control. To grieve, and to grieve bitterly, according as the occasion is one of distressing trial, is, as has been said, a tribute to nature on which religion does not frown. But to abandon one's-self to grief, to indulge the passion without attempt at restraint, is plainly a course unworthy of a being, whom, in all circumstances, conscience and sense of duty ought to admonish, and trust in God ought to sustain. To concentrate the attention on what has been lost, so as to acknowledge no worth and take no satisfaction in blessings which remain; to suffer our impatience to vent itself in murmurs against God, or a sullen or irritable deportment to our associates; to refuse to be comforted, and permit sorrow to put an end to our usefulness, or prey upon our health or life;—these are intemperate expressions of grief, which a Christian cannot approve in another, nor allow in his own practice.

But how is moderation in grief to be

maintained? For it is easy to say that we should be resigned; the difficulty is, how to acquire that state of feeling. Doubtless it is to be maintained in part by consideration of the criminality of an opposite course, evincing as this does such a want of self-command, and such a want of gratitude for God's continued favors, and of confidence in his parental love. But it must be owned that the tempest of the feelings is not at once to be stilled, by reflecting merely that we do wrong to suffer it to rage. What we are bound to do, we are equally bound to seek and use the means of doing; and the speediest and most effectual way to recover peace of mind, when the obligation of that endeavor is felt, seems to be, to trace out and contemplate the causes which exist for acquiescence. Accordingly, I know of nothing more characteristic of a Christian mourner, than a readiness to see, and rate at their due worth, whatever consolations may be found. Is our affliction such as is common to man, or have we long had merciful notice of its approach? We ought not to magnify it "as if some strange thing had happened." Is the blessing denied or withdrawn, compensated by other blessings; or had we a protracted enjoyment of it before we were called to resign it; or are we, after all, more privileged on the whole than most or than many of our associates? Let us not shut our eyes to this, but own it and be thankful for it. At all events, that we have reason and revelation, and may have a hope of everlasting life, whatever else we may have, or want, or lose, is enough, one would think, to forbid us to say that we have no resource for happiness left. Whatever we have possessed, it was God who gave it; and he remains as able as he then was in some way to supply its place, or indemnify us with other bounties, or otherwise reconcile us to our privation. Whatever we may have suffered, he is able,—this is a truth which perplexes our imaginations for the future, but our experience vouches it for the past,—he is able to make it co-operate with all the arrangements of his kind providence for our good; and if, as we sometimes might seem to desire, the management of our concerns could be transferred from his hands to our own, how plain is it that we should soon be driven to ask, as the greatest of boons, that he would resume the trust. However we may have been tried, it has not been as he was, who for our sakes "endured such contradiction of sinners against himself;" and to him we may always look when we are tempted to be weary and faint in our minds. Such considerations are but a few of the most general ones, to which in its adversity the religious mind has recourse, to chasten its tumultuous emotions. Special considerations of a similar tendency belong to each individual visitation of sorrow. If we will be blind to them, we may sorrow without hope. But if, as our duty is, we take pains to search them out and do them justice, our grief may be keen, but it will hardly be indulged beyond all bounds of reason.

To have learned to grieve without extravagance will be a preparation for other duties of the afflicted, of which I proceed, secondly, to name the maintenance of a benevolent interest in others.

It has been often mentioned as a good use of affliction, that it softens the heart; and that tendency it doubtless has, when its action is regulated by a Christian spirit. But immoderate grief is in its nature a selfish, an anti-social passion. The mourner who does not feel that the obligations of a Christian are upon him, is tempted to think too much of the immunities of his condition, and, along with this, to judge very erroneously of its claims. As to the latter, conceiving that excess of grief proves great intensity of affection, he refuses to control his sorrow lest he should seem to wrong an attachment which he knows was cordial and devoted. A heathen moralist could reason better than this. "No evil," said the eloquent Roman, "hath happened to my departed friend. Whatever it be, it concerns only myself; and to be severely afflicted at one's own misfortunes is a proof not of love to our friends, but to ourselves." And though this mode of arguing certainly does not show that grief on the like occasion is unreasonable, it does show that we cannot reasonably indulge it to extravagance, on the ground of any disinterested sentiments which it proves. And if we are assured that others will be tender, in their blame of us, for any weak and selfish surrender to our griefs, this is the worst of reasons why we should be tender of ourselves. There has much been very mischievously written, in books of poetry and fiction, and elsewhere, going to represent inconsolable sorrow, forever brooding on its painful recollections, and withdrawn by them from other cares, in an amiable point of view; and the young and sentimental have been often betrayed by that outrageous representation. A Christian cannot acknowledge the least justness in it. The immoderate passion of grief, as far as its excess is voluntary, as far as it is to be traced to indulgence, is to be regarded in the same light with other immoderate passions. Its victims are to be pitied, but certainly they are not to be justified, much less to be admired.

What is a culpable excess in grief, it may be difficult, or impossible, for any but the individual concerned to know. Men are not formed alike; and an excessive sensibility, constituting a sort of moral impotence in this respect, has seemed sometimes as if it were a part of the original constitution. Also, there may be conceived a complication of sorrows which would threaten to enervate the stoutest, and overwhelm the best fortified Christian hearts. But, apart from the large and just allowance due to such peculiar causes, he who should be in the way to die, as it is said, of a broken heart,—however others, in their indulgence, may regard him,—has scarcely a right to regard himself with more respect, than if he were falling a victim to any other intemperance. An unrestrained passion,—let me call it, for plainness' sake, by a harder name, an ungoverned temper,—is wearing upon his strength. It may be now too late for him to resist its ravages, but so it is in other cases of inordinate self-indulgence, which excite less commiseration. The fault was in not beginning the work of self-control in season. If, indeed, he struggled with all his might, but ineffectually, he stands acquitted in his conscience and before his judge. If he did not so struggle, till, through his own fault, it was too late, he has been his own destroyer.

Yes, no one has a right, because he has been afflicted, to suppose that he may surrender himself to unprofitable and selfish grief. If this were admissible, and every one who was entitled to the privilege were to claim it, how many do we suppose would remain in the world, who were under obligation to concern themselves for others' happiness? That the afflicted should appeal to others for sympathy,—for I need not repeat that these remarks have application only to cases of wilful perseverance, of self-indulgence in lamentation,—is not only right; it is even benevolent. It is an acceptable mark of their confidence in others' good will. But it is not right that they should retire within themselves, and on the ground that they are so disheartened by their calamities, dispense themselves from all interest in others' concerns; and still less is it right that they should inflict perhaps the worst pang on the hearts of those who share their sorrow, by cherishing bitter regrets which they will not permit to be consoled. Some time of solitude is reasonably allowed to the afflicted to compose their spirits; and there are scenes of ordinary action from which, if there be no distinct call of duty, they may for a further time be excused from shrinking. But the dispensation thus created from the duties of one's place in life, is one of no long duration. It should rather be the aim to go back to them as soon as the needful strength can be recovered; and the afflicted disciple of that man of sorrows, whose sorrows never withheld him from the work of doing good, will be impatient to give abundant proof, that, in being made to feel for himself, he has been led to feel more sensibly for others. Even to the earliest period of his recovered self-command, there is a favorite ministry of benevolence peculiarly appropriate; for the afflicted are the best consolers of affliction. Their communion, if it be in other respects what it may be, is worth more to a mourner than that of the best of other friends.

A third counsel belonging to our subject is given by the wise man, where he says, "In the day of adversity, consider."

The day of adversity is a time especially favorable to that serious reflection, which to all may be so useful, and of which many stand so much in need. Gay views of life are hasty and superficial; and such are the views to which in a course of uninterrupted prosperity the mind is liable to be confined. It is apt then to be giddy, and so to look at nothing steadily; to be hurried from object to object, and so to look at nothing long; to be confident in its judgments, so as to give them no fair opportunity to be right; to be flattered, which is but another name for being deluded. The view of seriousness and humility,—states of mind which affliction favors,—is likeliest to be the view of truth; and if adversity too has its occasions of false judgment, and a depressed mind, no less than an elate one, may discern objects through a distorting medium, still we shall be the better assured of a true result for comparing observations made from different points of view. The reflections of adversity certainly tend to reduce many things to their true proportions, which may have figured before us with a magnified importance. They do strip "the worshipped pageantry of pride" of much of its attraction. They do show us, that there is something we need more than the gratifications of the passing hour, and something beyond what wealth can purchase. They do expose the pretensions of every thing external to the soul to confer a trustworthy happiness, and display the worth of the treasures which are lodged within it.

The thought of our sins in prosperity is apt to be a transient and unaffecting thought. In our adversity the consideration of them comes to us with solemnity and power. Our feelings already harmonizing with the sentiments which they ought to prompt, they are seen in their reality; they make their inexcusableness and their danger known. Our obligations too then present themselves in an impressive form. We find ourselves thrown on our own resources for peace of mind. We are made to feel that an approving conscience, and, what naturally attends it, a tranquil trust in God and hope of his approbation, are what we have cause most to covet or to prize, as the case may be; and the holy life which wins them reveals itself to us for what it is,—the one thing demanding our diligent and earnest pursuit.

But the consideration most directly

pressed on the afflicted by the state to which they have been brought, is, of what use does it admit for the furtherance of their spiritual interests. I do not say, for what purpose has it been ordained to them; for this is a question which they cannot expect completely to resolve, though, if they use it well, one purpose for which it will then appear to have been sent is, to make them better men. The proper subject of concern in any posture of circumstances, is, not that it has occurred;—that it has occurred is now a determined and unalterable thing;—but, how to make the best of those circumstances—what use to fix on, to be made of things as they stand. The afflicted are to consider, what temper of mind their condition demands of them to manifest; what virtues it gives them facilities for cultivating, and how its aid may be secured for that use; how they may so demean themselves in their trial as to please God, and to serve the cause of the religion of Jesus, as others in time past have done, of whose example of patient endurance of calamity they are themselves now experiencing the benefit. Revolving such considerations, and carrying their lessons into practice, how many have afterwards found occasion to say, that affliction was a genuine and distinguished blessing to them. The best characters we have known are such as have been formed under its discipline. There are examples of an excellence, which, without training of this nature in some form, does not seem capable of being attained. An old philosopher said, of a voyage in which he suffered shipwreck, and lost his earthly all, that it was the most successful voyage he ever made, for it led him to renounce other pursuits for the pursuit of wisdom and virtue. How many Christians are there who trace acquisitions, which now incomparably above all others they prize, to considerations suggested, resolutions formed, feelings chastened, under circumstances which, at the time, they regarded only as the most distressingly disastrous.

Once more; "is any afflicted, let him pray." "He is a miserable man," says one, "who is afflicted and cannot or will not pray."

Let the afflicted pray, because he much needs what the world cannot give him, and what God, whom he addresses, is able and ready to give. Let him pray, because the very act of prayer will tranquillize his spirit, and raise it above passionate sorrow, and inspire it with new hope. Let the afflicted pray, because prayer is the natural language of confidence in the best of friends, and that confidence will grow and brighten while it is expressed. When we draw nigh to God to ask comfort of him, and strength to sustain the day of his visitation, it cannot be but that every feeling as if he had wronged us, as if he had dealt hardly with us, in the trial we endure, will be banished from our minds. Let the afflicted pray, because in that season when the mind in its desolation has recourse to the power which alone can give it support, and the love that knows no limit, prayer has a peculiar fervor, is a peculiarly deep and earnest breathing of the affections; the worth of the privilege of prayer is more than ever revealed, and the pleasures of devotion are permanently endeared to the soul. Let the afflicted pray, because, as has been seen, their situation imposes on them duties; duties, through which they may advance their own spiritual interests, please God, profit others, and serve the cause of Christ; and to acquit themselves well of these, they need guidance and strength from above, whence prayer will bring strength and guidance down. Let the afflicted pray, finally, because the great example of sufferers, Jesus, prayed. And let them endeavor to pray with some portion of his spirit. Submission is the Christian's divine peace, which passeth understanding; and if the prayer which breathes it do not bring down, as it did to the Savior, a strengthening angel, it will itself do an angel's office to the stricken heart.

THE MOURNER BLESSED.

DEEM not that they are blessed alone,
  Whose days a peaceful tenor keep;
The God who loves our race has shown
  A blessing for the eyes that weep.

The light of smiles shall beam again
  From lids that now o'erflow with tears,
And weary hours of woe and pain
  Are earnests of serener years.

Oh there are days of hope and rest
  For every dark and troubled night!
And grief may bide, an evening guest,
  But joy shall come with early light.

And ye, who o'er a friend's low bier
  Now shed the bitter drops like rain,
Hope that a brighter, happier sphere
  Will give him to your arms again.

Nor let the good man's trust depart,
  Though life its common gifts deny;
Nor hopeless sorrow break the heart,
  That, spurned of men, fears not to die.

For God hath marked each anguished day,
  And numbered every secret tear;
And heaven's long age of bliss shall pay
  For all his children suffer here.

CONSOLATION.

When the clouds of desolation
  Gather o'er my naked head,
And my spirit's agitation
  Knows not where to turn or tread;
When life's gathering storms compel me
  To submit to wants and woes,
Who shall teach me, who shall tell me
  Where my heart may find repose?

God and Father! thou did'st give me
  Sorrow for my portion here;
But thy mercy will not leave me
  Helpless, struggling with despair;
For to thee, when sad and lonely,
  Unto thee alone I turn,
And to thee, my Father! only
  Look for comfort when I mourn.

Nor in vain—for light is breaking
  'Midst the sorrows, 'midst the storms;
And methinks I see awaking
  Heavenly hopes and angel forms;
And my spirit waxes stronger,
  And my trembling heart is still;
And my bosom doubts no longer
  Thine inexplicable will.

THE DANGERS OF ADVERSITY.

No subject of exhortation is oftener chosen by the divine and the moralist than the dangers of prosperity and the blessings of adversity. It is a good subject, and deserves all that can be said upon it; but should not the reverse of the picture be sometimes held up to view? There is little need, perhaps, to dwell much on the moral advantages of prosperity in order to make it desired, as such a state needs no new attractions to render it beautiful in the eyes and welcome to the heart of man; but it seems desirable to point out to the child of immortality the dangers which beset the path of sorrow; a path which, though thorny to the feet and obstructed to the view, is generally represented as enlightened by the day-spring from on high, and infallibly tending to heights of holiness and peace. Do we sufficiently reflect that such is not its universal tendency? Are we aware that adversity has slain its thousands, though prosperity may have destroyed its ten thousands? It behooves us to be careful that, while we desire and aim at advancement in holiness, we are not lost through want of circumspection. While we guard against the snares of wealth, ease, and worldly privileges, let us not flatter ourselves that, as soon as sorrow overtakes us, we must necessarily become more worthy of the love of the Father who chasteneth us, that our hearts must necessarily be purified, and our affections elevated.

Though sorrow may soften the heart, it may also harden it; it may expand or contract the affections; it may bring us to God or alienate us from him, according to our previous habits of mind, or to our course of action under the pressure of new circumstances. Instead of believing that the bitter draught of sorrow will assuredly confer immortality, we must bear in mind that it will act according to our preparation for its operation; it may renovate our powers; it may restore our vigor, and infuse new life into our spiritual frame; but it may also exert a relaxing and benumbing influence, and unawares lay us prostrate in eternal death. If we do not endeavor to discern what influence the operations of Providence ought to have on our character, and strive to subject ourselves duly to them, we may expect in vain the precious results for which we look with confidence. Some results will be produced, perhaps valuable, perhaps noxious, but our expectations will be disappointed unless we anxiously observe, and, as far as possible, carefully direct the process. It is not every lump of earth which will yield gold in the crucible, and it is not every mind which will come forth from its fiery trial adorned with solid and shining virtues.

But though adversity may benefit some minds more than others, it has its dangers for all. That which is oftenest pointed out is distrust of the goodness of God. This is however, in our opinion, by no means the greatest. In a Christian country like this, where every sabbath renews the praises of the Father of mercies, where preachers abound to display instances of his goodness, where through the whole range of its literature, from the volume which invites little children to "bless God, for he is very good," to that which appeals to his "glorious works" to show that he is the "parent of good," express acknowledgments of the benignity of Providence are found in every page,—a belief in this benignity is so early formed and so strongly maintained, that it usually stands the shock of adverse events, and dwells, actively or passively, in the mind through life. It is almost as uncommon, in this age and country, to meet with a denial of the unalterable goodness of God, as a doubt of his existence. Those who are practically resigned to his will and those who are not, equally acknowledge the justice and mercy of that will.

A much greater danger appears to us to be a tendency in the sufferer to imagine that he is an object of God's peculiar favor; that he is exalted in the sight of God and man by his mere suffering, independently of the effect which it may have on his character. Where this fatal notion once obtains entrance, presumption usurps the place of humility; the spirit *condescends* to receive the inflictions of its parent, and congratulates itself on its submission. It looks round to see what the world thinks of its resignation, and from that moment it becomes the slave of the world.

The world takes upon itself to prescribe rules for the demeanor of those who are under the pressure of sorrow; and hence is another snare for the weak and the worldly. The same events produce such different effects on different minds, that the innocent pleasures in which one mourner finds a welcome solace, may call up associations too powerful for the fortitude of another. But the world has one rule for all, and he who does not obey it must expect to meet its censure and its scorn. The humble sufferer who believes not that his feelings are of consequence enough to interfere with the comfort of others, who suppresses his sighs that the smiles of those around him may not be checked, who goes everywhere, and sees every one, and leaves no accustomed duty unperformed, is too often censured as wanting feeling; while he who shuts himself up, or is never seen but in gloom and tears, and who requires peculiar consideration for his situation from every one he sees and every company he enters, is held up to admiration as an example of refined sensibility, and is honored with the praise of being "a true mourner." The world *will* judge; but he who submits his feelings and conduct to its judgment, takes upon him a yoke which will grow heavier with each day of his life in this world, and which may deliver him over to a still worse destiny in another. Any one who has studied the structure of the human mind is aware, that there is no such thing as permanent, utter misery. Our associations are so complex, the pleasant are so mixed with the painful, the power of external objects over them is so great, and the tendency of the mind to call up pleasurable and consolatory thoughts is so strong, that no efforts of our own, from a regard to the opinion of the world, or any other motive, can long depress the elasticity of the soul. If such be the happy bent of our nature, why should it be counteracted? If we possess the power of enjoying innocent pleasures, our true wisdom is to seek them, whatever our circumstances may be, and whatever the world may think of our sensibilities.

It need scarcely be suggested how careful we should be not to censure our fellow-sufferers for shrinking from efforts which are beneficial to ourselves, or to judge of their conduct by our own, be the apparent similarity of the circumstances ever so striking. While we feel that the world may as well attempt to fathom the ocean, or reach the uttermost parts of the earth, as to compass our griefs or estimate our consolations, we must guard ourselves against a similar presumption, though our own discipline may have enlightened our eyes and instructed our judgments.

Two other dangers next present themselves to our notice, opposite in their character, but equally formidable. There is much fear that the soul which has suffered much should become callous; and this peril may be enhanced by the very tendency of the mind, (to turn to pleasant thoughts wherever they can be found,) which has been mentioned as one of the happiest circumstances of our nature. It is a privilege which the Father of mercies has conferred on his rational offspring; and while it serves as an alleviation of our griefs and a means of refreshment and invigoration to the soul, it can be subservient only to good: but when we make use of it to turn our minds from serious reflection, to escape from Him who would purify us by salutary discipline, we convert our privilege into a curse. If, when we find our hopes disappointed and our blessings withdrawn, we can find a refuge from regret in the trifling interests of the world, if we play the truant to avoid our punishment, we must not congratulate ourselves on bearing it well; but should rather mourn that what ought to be the most efficacious means of grace does but harden our hearts, accumulate new perils upon our heads, and augment the heavy reckoning which futurity has in store against us. To this danger the strong and high spirit is most exposed: to its opposite—timidity, the gentle and humble soul is peculiarly liable.

But few words are necessary here. Those who have known what real sorrow is, know also what it is to tremble at every breath, to dread every change, to strain the aching sight to discern what new evils lie in the clouded future, to have a superstitious, unacknowledged feeling that every effort will end in disappointment, every blessing prove a snare, every acquisition give place to bereavement. They scarcely dare approach the streams of God's bounty lest they should be defiled with blood, and are ready to refuse to taste the fruits which he showers into their lap, lest they should find them dust and bitter ashes. This timidity may, for a while, consist with a desire to acquiesce in the appointments of Providence; but if not timely checked, it will lead through the gradations of despondency, ingratitude, and insensibility, to atheism, speculative and practical.

Many more are the snares into which the unwary may fall in a state which is too often thought to be one of peculiar safety. But those which remain will suggest themselves to the mind of the reader under some of the preceding heads. The principal of those on which we cannot now enlarge are dreaminess,—living in a world of imagination and sentiment—and listlessness in the performance of necessary but irksome duties. The first arises from the error of fancying that the subjects of discipline are the objects of God's peculiar favor, in a strictly literal sense; the last, from the selfishness against which, in various forms, we have been warning the reader. It is so evidently hostile to all improvement, so fatal to the hopes which ought to be the Christian's chief treasure, and all arguments against it are so obvious and so common, that the mere mention of it is sufficient here.

Of all these perils, those are the most formidable which endanger the sincerity and ingenuousness of the heart. But the soul may be lost where sincerity and resignation both exist; want of circumspection alone may be fatal. How important is this truth to us!

A man may mourn most deeply and most truly; he may earnestly desire to exercise resignation; he may, with the utmost sincerity, declare to himself that he does not wish one circumstance of his lot to be altered, and yet fall into snares as dangerous as any which can be found in the flowery paths of prosperity. He may arise in the morning, and pray with real devotion for resignation to bear, and strength to support, and then go forth, satisfied that the blessing of God is on him, and that he must necessarily be benefited by his trial. But when he enters the bustling scenes of the world, he fears to surrender himself to his accustomed impulses of activity, and to his long-formed habits of employment. He is ashamed if he find that the objects before him have beguiled him of his grief for a while; he asks himself if the innocent enjoyment into which he was beginning to enter is not inconsistent with the regret which he owes to the memory of the friend he has lost, or the sympathy which is due to those with whom he is suffering. He remembers that he is in affliction, and has a vague idea that a peculiar frame of thought and manners must be maintained for some time after the blow has fallen. The consciousness of peculiar circumstances hangs upon him, and makes him look in every face for condolence, in every occurrence for consideration to his feelings, in every word for sympathy. He has heard and read so much of the experience of persons under trial, and knows so well how their demeanor is made a subject of speculation, that he believes it necessary to relate his own feelings, and to watch that his own behavior accords with his circumstances. If he writes a letter to a friend, he fills his sheet with his thoughts of resignation; he tells of his consolations, his hopes, and the blessings which remain to him; and if he finds himself stopping his pen to choose his expressions, if he detects himself *painting* with words, if a suspicion flits across his mind that he is exciting his feelings in order to write, rather than writing to give a natural relief to his feelings, he recurs to the old impression that some record of his present state should remain, and that it is for the glory of religion that he should show how great and how various are her consolations. Thus he passes the day, desiring that the will of God should be his will, and believing that it is so; but, in reality, thinking only of himself, and living only to himself. If, in the silent watches of the night, sad thoughts arise, and the tender remembrance of lost blessings comes to awaken the deepest emotions of his soul, he waters his pillow with tears, and indulges the anguish of a wounded spirit; still assuring himself that he does not and will not repine, and that this grief is only the fitting tribute of faithful affection. Again he rises, with an aching head and a heavy heart, wearied and enervated, and more engrossed with himself than ever, though he may again pray, and pray with sincerity, "Thy will be done."

What are the consequences of such a course of feeling and action as this? What but daily increasing selfishness; morbid feelings which, instead of retaining or deepening their intensity, must induce insensibility; a gradual forgetfulness of God and disregard of duty; a growing craving for the sympathy, the approbation, the applause of others; a paramount desire of being interesting, and the sacrifice of one thing after another, of *all*, for the sake of being so? Can any one say that this is an exaggerated picture? Happy is he who has never known such a victim to the dangers of adversity; but happier is he who has resisted and overcome similar perils, who has properly estimated his blessings while he possessed them, and become better by resigning them!

The means of such improvement are natural to some minds, easy to others, and attainable by all. The grand rule is to look to *principles*, and to leave *feelings* to take care of themselves. This rule includes every thing. Principle will lead the mourner to refer all to God; principle will oblige him to forget himself, and will suggest to him continual occasions of doing good to others. Principle will teach him that affliction is not intended to set him apart from others, but to enlighten his views of his relation to them, to exalt his affections towards them, to animate his efforts in their behalf. He must, sometimes, notwithstanding his endeavors to forget himself, feel what an aching void sorrow has left in his heart; but, instead of turning his view inwards to behold the desolation there, he will look abroad with a searching eye on the varied aspects which life presents to him: he will gather together all the images of peace, hope, and joy, which he can lay hold on, to supply the cravings of his affections. He will go forth into the world from the house of mourning, calm and erect, prepared to abide its storms, and ready to welcome its sunshine. He will have smiles for the infant, and a heart open to its little joys; he will have cheerfulness for the aged, and a ready hand to help their infirmities; he will have words of encouragement and of warning for the young, and a watchful eye to protect their interests; he will rejoice in their brilliant hopes as if they were his own, and will grieve for their destruction as if the loss were his. While he can "rejoice with those who rejoice," he will bury his peculiar griefs in his own bosom: when called on to "weep with those that weep," he will speak of himself only so far as to tell where he found the supports and comforts which, by the blessing of God, have been his. He does not desire to shroud his mind in mystery; it is there, clear and transparent, for all to look into who choose: he only wishes that the gusts of passion should not ruffle, or the clouds of despondency overshadow it. His regard to duty imposes on him the care of his health and of his tranquillity. The works of God are his study abroad; the word of God employs him at home. He keeps his powers in full exercise all day, and at night he seeks and obtains rest; or, if darkness and silence exert on him their peculiar influence of calling up the shadows of departed joys, he endeavors to be grateful that these joys *were* his; he estimates the privileges they have afforded him, and numbers the blessings he has left; he listens to the assurances of faith, that all these and many more are laid up for him as a treasure in heaven; and his soul glows with the resolution, that where his treasure is, there his heart shall be also. It requires no great discernment to trace the further progress of his discipline. We need only look at some who have thus trodden their thorny path, and then we may see how he will daily advance in the love of God and man, and in fitness for his heavenly destiny. He will attain the heights of holiness, and will encourage many to follow him thither; for he will say, by example, though not in words, "Be of good cheer; I have overcome the world."

Where one such sufferer is seen, we may rejoice in the power of religion, tended and cherished by adversity: when we see several, a whole family, submitting to the will of God, and working out their own and each other's salvation, in patience and self-oblivion, we may glory that such a sanctuary abides on earth for the spirit of holiness to dwell in. Such a family are God's peculiar people, and if their obedience to his commands will not avail to exclude the angel of chastisement from their abode, a milder presence will soon follow to repair the devastation, and to whisper the gracious benediction, "Peace be to this house." Peace will remain with them; will rest upon them when they go out and when they come in, when they lie down and when they rise up, in the dwelling and in the field, in the house of God, and in the intercourses of the world.

TRUST IN DIVINE LOVE.

O let my trembling soul be still,
  While darkness veils this mortal eye,
And wait thy wise, thy holy will:
  Wrapt yet in fears and mystery,
I cannot, Lord! thy purpose see;
Yet all is well—since ruled by thee.

When, mounted on thy clouded car,
  Thou send'st thy darker spirits down,
I can discern thy light afar,
  Thy light sweet beaming through thy frown;
And, should I faint a moment, then
I think of thee, and smile again.

So trusting in thy love, I tread
  The narrow path of duty on:
What though some cherished joys are fled?
  What though some flattering dreams are gone?
Yet purer, brighter joys remain:
Why should my spirit then complain?

THE PROMISE OF JESUS.

"Come unto me, all ye that labor and are heavy laden, and I will give you rest."

Thou of the heavy heart, his promise hear,
Thou in whose cup earth's ills are deeply rife,
Turn unto him without a dread, a fear,
Turn unto him, and he will give thee life.

There is but One can keep thee in the hour,
The darkest hour of sorrow's troubled day;
Then when the tempests o'er thy spirit lower,
Turn to thy God!—oh bend the knee and pray!

The "bruised reed" in mercy he will bind,
He will not crush the heart that "once knew strife"—
But in his home a welcome all will find;
Turn unto him, and he will give thee life!

THE BELIEVER'S HOPE.

How dark, how desolate
Would many a moment be,
Could we not spring
On hope's bright wing,
O God! to heaven and thee!

Life is a prison cell
We are doomed to occupy,
In which confined,
The restless mind
Pines, pants for liberty.

And sometimes streaks of light
And sunny beams we see;
They shine so bright
Through sorrow's night,
They needs must come from thee.

Say, shall a morning dawn
When prison-days are o'er,
Whose smiling ray
Shall wake a day,
That night shall cloud no more?

Blest hope! and sure as blest;
Life's shades of misery
Shall soon be past,
And joy at last
Waft us to heaven and thee.

THE USES OF AFFLICTION.

THAT happiness, which is fed only by the world's smiles, by scenes of uninterrupted gayety, is delusive and false. The soul has a happiness, which need not be destroyed by the passing clouds that overshadow man's earthly pilgrimage. I would show this, and would teach, if I could, that from scenes which cause the worldly mind to mourn in hopelessness the soul may gather strength and permanent peace. I would gather unwithering garlands even from the tomb, to overspread and cheer the path of life. I would show that it is good to be afflicted, and would thus make even the sorrows of earth minister to the comfort, as they may minister to the improvement of the undying spirit. I would produce the conviction, that all is good in the purposes of an infinite Father, that all may contribute to the soul's health, strength, peace, and immortal happiness.

But are afflictions *necessarily* conducive to man's happiness? We answer, *no.* They are good in the purposes of God, but whether they shall be good to any individual depends upon himself. They are part of a moral discipline, and their efficacy depends upon the free action of the soul itself. The gifts of God's providence are good; but how many abuse them, and convert his blessings into the instruments of personal degradation and ruin! Amid the frowns of the world, in the disappointment of earthly hopes, by the struggles of poverty, some have formed characters of exalted excellence, and have shown forth the power of the soul to rise above earthly trials, to gain purity and power by the storms which beat upon it. Some have, under such circumstances, borne the nearest resemblance ever exhibited on earth to him, who had not where to lay his head. Others, again, have withered under the trials of life, have let go their hold on heaven, forgotten their immortal destiny, yielded to sin, and now plead the discouragements in their path as an apology for their moral ruin and spiritual death. Some too have risen from the bed of sickness, or come forth from the chamber of móurning, with holier purposes, with purer affections, and a more cheerful and sustaining piety; others again have passed through such scenes, and come from them in discouragement, or with a more decided selfishness, or with a complaining, testy, distrustful habit of mind, abusing the world, yet clinging to it with most exclusive devotion, and pouring contempt upon God, and Christ, and every emotion of a confiding, affectionate piety.

Whether afflictions be good for any individual, must depend, under God, upon the manner in which they are received and employed. They will be good only so far as they are made instrumental in turning the bad man from his iniquities, and impressing upon his soul the image of his Maker; or as they give to the good man new ardor in duty, and a fuller confidence in God, urge him onward in his course, bring him into more intimate communion with the spiritual world, and impart brighter visions of the glories hereafter to be revealed.

We now proceed to illustrate the tendency of affliction to minister to man's spiritual and eternal happiness.

What is requiste to bring religion with a life-giving power to the souls of men? It is attention, deep, practical attention. "My people will not consider," was the complaint urged by God himself against the disobedient. Religion meets a want of the soul, which nothing else can meet, which nothing else can supply. Religion is the one thing needful; needful to give harmony to the elements which compose man's moral nature, needful to his virtue, needful to his peace, needful to his spiritual progress, needful to that hope which is an anchor to the soul. But religion is nothing as a mere name, a mere abstraction; it is nothing except as the spirit of man firmly grasps its truths, acts upon them, lives by them, and rejoices in them. But this can be done only by deep, practical attention. The allurements of the world, its busy cares, its engrossing interests, tend to render him a stranger to his spiritual capacities and wants, to turn away the thoughts from the world within, to fix the affections upon objects as transitory as the flower which blooms and fades in a day. Religion is neglected; the world is every thing; and the soul is famished. Place this endangered being, thus treacherous to his own happiness, upon the bed of sickness. Let him feel the pressure of disease, and experience the rush of thought which breaks in upon him; and what then are things transitory and perishing? Wealth, ambition, pleasure will not, cannot satisfy him amid the paroxysms of pain and the withering of every earthly hope. The soul must experience unmitigated anguish, if it cannot hold communion with the infinite Spirit, if it cannot look forward to treasures enduring as its own immortal nature. But at such a season attention is fixed upon Jesus, who came into the world to guide the spirits of men to intimate communion with the infinite Father and with the spiritual world, to open the treasures of God's love and the enduring riches of the immortal mind. Religion becomes an object of fixed, practical, grateful attention.

Is not this the tendency and design of afflictions? Then it is good to be afflicted; good for the pious man, as it deepens his religious impressions, quickens his sensibilities, and brightens his hopes; good for the careless and irreligious man, as it may save his soul from death. The good man will bless God for his trials; and oh how guilty is that man who perverts the very means of healing the diseases of his soul, of redeeming him from guilt, and making him an heir of eternal glory,—who rises from the bed of sickness, or comes from the chamber of mourning, to blunt the sensibilities there excited by earthly turmoil and guilty pleasures, or to murmur and complain, to cling more closely to the world, and, like the soldier who has escaped where thousands have fallen around him, to regard himself as the son of destiny, and proof against the weapons of death!

Afflictions are adapted not only to awaken attention to religion, but to prepare the mind to receive and love its spirit. There is an obtuseness of moral feeling generated by a familiar intercourse with the world. Vice is seen in a thousand forms, and by familiarity with it delicacy of feeling is blunted, and moral discrimination becomes less acute. I cannot describe to you the state of feeling produced by any severe affliction. You must experience it to understand it fully. But what is the tendency of being brought to feel that earthly things cannot satisfy the soul's wants; that you are in the presence of a holy God; and that you may soon stand before the bar of Jesus

Christ? I would point you to the testimony of those who have been accustomed to listen to the accents of the sick and dying, of those who have been called to minister to the mourner's sorrows, of those who have been recently instructed in the school of affliction. They will tell you that such scenes produce a delicacy of moral feeling, a shrinking back from all iniquity, and a panting for purity, which it is worth worlds to preserve amid the collisions and temptations of life. This is the very state of feeling which is congenial with the spirit of the gospel, and which renders it the welcome instrument of heaven to the soul; the very state which gives a sympathy with the holy Jesus, and renders man capable of enjoying the riches of God's love.

By affliction, also, man is enabled to determine what is truly of vital importance in religion. It is wonderful to behold what power the severe pressure of sorrow has in simplifying the religious faith, and fixing the mind on those great truths which all Christians admit. He who listens to the sentiments and prayers of a single-hearted Christian in the hour of severe trial, will find his soul clinging to these truths, which all good men love, and clinging to them as alone furnishing strength and comfort.

Afflictions, in the next place, teach the love of God, submission to his will, gratitude for his favors, and a cheerful trust in his mercy. These are high Christian virtues, without which the heart must be a stranger to permanent peace. But it may be deemed little less than a perfect paradox to assert that these virtues are taught in the school of affliction. I am aware that they are not always learned there, that among the tried and distressed are often heard bitter complaints, is often witnessed the sorrow of the world, which worketh death. But if these virtues are not cherished in the school of affliction, they seldom are cherished anywhere. Look into the history of man, as it exhibits itself constantly before your eyes.

Where do you witness the purest love of God, the most heartfelt gratitude to him, the most profound submission to his will, and the most cheerful trust in his mercy? You will not usually find these high qualities of character in those whose progress in life has been one of almost unchecked prosperity, who have had no severe struggles with adversity, whose health has never been interrupted, whose plans have seldom been frustrated, and to whom the gifts of Providence have been granted in rich profusion. Among such persons we too often witness self-confidence, pride, hardness of heart, vain display, and, if not open impiety, a melancholy insensibility to religion, a clinging to the earth, a forgetfulness of God and heaven. It is among those whose souls have been severely disciplined, who have wrestled frequently with trials, among those who to the carnally minded seem to have the least cause for gratitude, that you will find the highest spiritual qualities, the most perfect harmony of character, the most entire love of God, the most unwavering trust in his mercy, and the most cheerful acquiescence in his will.

How is this fact to be explained? Mere suffering in itself cannot awaken love, or inspire gratitude or confidence toward the being who inflicts it. It is kindness that awakens love, and, when united with wisdom and power, produces confidence and submission. How is it then that these most cheerful virtues are brought out and perfected by the severest discipline? It is by fixing the attention upon God, and opening the heart to his goodness. There are no unmitigated sufferings in human life. All that is requisite to call forth love to God, gratitude for his mercies, and submission to his will, is such a clear perception, such a deep feeling of this truth, as can be acquired only in the school of affliction. There the thoughts are forced in upon the soul itself, and elevated above this world of shadows. God is made present, the spiritual nature of man is more fully understood, and, on inquiring for comfort, the mourner finds abundant sources opened to him. He now sees what he had not seen before, that his past history has been but a display of the divine goodness towards him; in the present kindness of friends, in the cheerful face of nature, in the expressions of happiness on the countenances of the multitude around him, in the comforts of faith, and in the hope of endless joys, he feels that God is good, and becomes convinced that his present anguish, however mysterious in its appointment, must b intended for good, and will result in good. He learns the application of Christian principles to his own spiritual wants. He fathoms their meaning, and feels their power. Talk to him of suffering, and he is firm. Speak to him of mercies; his bosom heaves, and his tears flow. It is thus that he gains spiritual power, and lays deep the foundations of his happiness. Oh who, that feels the dangers of the world, who, that has any perception of the worth of the soul, who, that has felt the softening and elevating power of earthly trials, will not say that it is good for him that he has been afflicted?

Again, it is one part of the blessed ministry of affliction to cherish a tender sympathy with others in their trials, and to call forth an active and discriminating beneficence. Admit that there is no natural connection between continued prosperity and a devoted selfishness; yet how often are they seen united! Suppose that a man has great tenderness of feeling, yet never has had his sensibilities tried by severe suffering, how can he fully enter into the feelings and wants of those who are deeply afflicted? Imagination cannot paint to him in true colors the conflicts through which they are passing. He may pity them, and minister to them with a most compassionate spirit; but a perfect sympathy can belong to him only who has himself been tried. He alone who has been himself exposed to severe sickness, who has seen the world withering away, who has felt in near anticipation the breaking of dear connections, who has known how deeply the mind sympathizes with the body, and what phantoms play before it and distress it in its dreamy struggles, can fully sympathize with the sick; and he alone, with whom earth's dearest ties have been sundered, can come to the mourner with accents, and with expressions of countenance, which will reach the depths of his sorrowing soul, and impart solid comfort. These scenes not only give the power of becoming sons of consolation; but they awaken benevolent feelings, and bind man to man by the cords of love.

Once more; it pertains to the ministry of affliction to render man familiar with his own character, and with the foundation on which his hope of happiness is placed. Afflictions are trials of character as well as means of improvement. But on whose account is the trial instituted? Not surely on God's; for he knows before the trial what will be its issue. It must, therefore, be instituted on man's account,—

to show him what is the strength of his principles, what the complexion of his hope. The good man may often be in great anxiety with regard to his spiritual condition, the strength of his love to God, and the security of the foundation on which he rests. Trials come upon him; he still clings to God: thy press heavily; he is unshaken in his faith, and his hope brightens, as the clouds gather blackness over him. He perceives that there is strength within him, and, though it be small, he yet rejoices in it, and is prepared by his trials for more vigorous efforts to add to his spiritual graces. The bad man may have scoffed at religion, and ridiculed its fears and hopes; by severe affliction the clamor of earthly passions is for a moment hushed, and his thoughts are forced inward and onward. He finds within desolation, and in the prospect before him nothing but despair. He sees himself, for the first time, what he is. His moral sensibilities are touched; he cries to God for mercy; he goes to Jesus for salvation, and, in new affections, new purposes, and new principles, he lays the foundation of eternal happiness.

But it is not simply the individual sufferer that is benefited by afflictions. They have a wider scope of influence. I see, while the mother, surrounded by her domestic circle, is ministering to one of that circle prostrated by disease, the fountain of tenderness deepening in her own bosom. I see the group around her in holy sympathy with her. I see affections excited, which in future life are to cheer and bless the rising generations of men. I see in every place of sickness and of death the means of kindling the flame of love.

What then is the conclusion to which we are brought? That this is, on the whole, a happy world; and that its dark and fearful scenes have a most benevolent influence upon human happiness. There is not a deeper conviction in my own mind of any truth than of this, that man, constituted as he is, would be far less happy, were the discipline of affliction to be withdrawn, were he to be immortal upon the earth. Why then should we shrink from taking our part of the sufferings of human life; sufferings which are most intimately connected with the full glory and perfect bliss of the immortal spirit? No; let afflictions come; if dispensed by the hand of an infinite Father, they must be good in their purpose. It remains for us to say whether they shall be good for us in their effects.

TIME PASSING.

TIME is passing, time is passing,
  Bid thy restless heart be still;
Time is passing, time is passing,
  God will work his holy will.

He who raised the lofty mountain,
  He who painted every flower,
Will ne'er his wondrous work forsake,
  Nor leave thee at the trying hour.

For soon, ah soon, the time may come,
  That bears thee to thy home away,
That breaks the bonds of kindred love,
  And takes thee to the realms of day.

Though thy heart be torn by anguish,
  Though thy spirit sink to dust,
Time is passing, time is passing,
  Put in God thy fervent trust.

THE CHRISTIAN'S DEATH.

BEHOLD the western evening light!
  It melts in deeper gloom!

So calm the righteous sink away,
  Descending to the tomb.

The winds breathe low—the yellow leaf
  Scarce whispers from the tree!
So gently flows the parting breath,
  When good men cease to be.

How beautiful, on all the hills,
  The crimson light is shed!
'T is like the peace the dying gives
  To mourners round his bed.

How mildly on the wandering cloud
  The sunset beam is cast!
So sweet the memory left behind,
  When loved ones breathe their last.

And lo! above the dews of night
  The vesper star appears!
So faith lights up the mourner's heart,
  Whose eyes are dim with tears.

Night falls, but soon the morning light
  Its glories shall restore!
And thus the eyes that sleep in death
  Shall wake to close no more.

THE HOPE OF IMMORTALITY.

CHRISTIANITY has been properly denominated the guide to immortality; Jesus expressly styles himself the resurrection and the life. Christianity reveals a future life; and in this respect Jesus and his religion have done what has not been satisfactorily done by any other person or any other system of religious belief. On this interesting subject the words of nature are few; the analogy of the vegetable creation and the annual renewal of the earth may delight the imagination, but can hardly bring conviction to the understanding. Reason and philosophy find in the grave a barrier, which they cannot pass; and experience acknowledges her utter ignorance of the country beyond it, since it remains the bourn from whence no traveller returns. But while we anxiously inquire, to whom shall we go, the gospel beams on us with life and immortality. The doctrine of a future life is a prominent doctrine of Christianity; other considerations inspire only a shadowy hope, this gives a substantial assurance. As in Adam all die, even so in Christ shall all be made alive; as after the similitude of the parent of the human race all men die, so after the similitude of the Redeemer of the human race, all men shall be raised from the dead. The certainty of a future life is far from being all that Christianity has given us; the hope of a bare renewal of life would be a small boon; the gospel has done much more than this, and though it has not communicated to us all that perhaps our curiosity might prompt us to ask, yet it has taught sufficient to satisfy every reasonable wish.

First, it teaches that the coming life shall be without end; that the power of death will be completely abolished; that our life will exist under a new and improved form; that the soul, no longer encased in a frail and earthly tenement, shall be exempted from all susceptibility to disease and destruction, and clothed with perpetual health and vigor; this corruptible shall put on incorruption, this mortal immortality. Existing under a new form, it gives us reason to expect an enlargement of our faculties, new facilities for acquiring knowledge, extended opportunities of serving God, a nature exempt from error, folly, and sin, and a continual and accelerated progress in moral goodness. Further, it encourages the expectation of an intimate connection with those good beings, with whom it must be the first of pleasures and of privileges to be associated; of entering into the rest which remains for the people of God; and of joining the assembly and church of the first-born. It inspires the hope of being closely united to Jesus Christ and of free access to God; we shall then know him even as we are known. Though it has not particularly disclosed the place or mode of our future existence, yet it assures us that it will be in every respect an infinitely better life than the present, and surpassing any wishes that we can frame of it; the eye of man hath not seen, nor his ear heard, nor his heart conceived the things, which God hath prepared for them that love him.

Consider now the completeness of this hope.

Is it not sufficiently definite? Can we name any object of virtuous desire, which it does not embrace? In the prospect of a renewed existence, elevated above all fear of death, of a constitution not susceptible of infirmity, suffering or decay, of a nature exempt from error and sin; in the prospect of capacities superior to any which you now possess, or of which you can form a conception; in the prospect of endless progress in the most valuable knowledge and the purest virtue, of a permanent and close connection with the best beings in offices of mutual love and extended usefulness, of an intimate communion with Jesus, the blessed author and guide of your faith, and of a spiritual fellowship with the Deity, then the supreme object of your adoration, love, confidence, and obedience; in fine, in the prospect of a life, where every virtuous desire will be gratified, and every delightful anticipation realized, Christianity inspires a hope in every respect complete, and which may well be denominated "an anchor to the soul."

I make my appeal to personal experience as to the value and necessity of such a hope, to support us under the trials incident to our present condition.

Hope is the medicine of the soul, the cordial which animates and sustains us under the labors of life, which alleviates the severest afflictions, and which sheds an increased splendor over the fairest day of earthly prosperity. But the best hopes, which take their rise only from this world, and whose flight is restricted within the narrow range of earthly good, are totally inadequate to allay the fear of death, and to remove, or in any measure to mitigate, some of the heaviest sufferings to which we are here subjected. There are disappointments, which this world cannot compensate; losses, for which it can afford no substitute; sorrows, to which it brings no alleviation. If I had no hope beyond the present transient scene, I know not how I should sustain sorrows, which every day befal me; I know not what should support me under the numerous and distressing inroads, which death is daily making on the circle of my friends. "To me I confess, as one well describes the effect of death upon the heathen, to me death would have a terrible sound, and could not but be attended with a train of the most melancholy reflections. It would unavoidably mix with all my enjoyments and unavoidably allay and spoil their relish. It would be like a sword continually hanging over my head by a single hair; a spectre always haunting my abode; which, whatever some libertines might pretend, would cast a sudden damp on every joy, and leave no present gratification free from pain and uneasiness." I cannot envy that gloomy scepticism or that brutal insensibility, which regards such events unmoved. I would not wish to purchase relief with the extinction of memory, since in the always present recollection of departed friends, who deserved my respect and affection, I find a powerful stimulus to virtue, and a satisfaction, though melancholy, yet most refreshing to my wounded and aching bosom.

In these sentiments I think I utter only the sentiments of every virtuous and feeling heart. What words then can express the value of a religion, which dispels all anxiety, solicitude, and grief at the departure of our virtuous and Christian friends? What language can express the value of that blessed hope, which entereth into that state which is beyond the veil of death; whither the forerunner, the guide and prince of life, the conqueror of death, even Jesus, has himself entered in glory and triumph?

Christian father and mother! when you have deposited in the grave the child of your affection and confidence and hope, perhaps the son whose virtues and talents and manly qualities were your pride and delight, or the daughter who clung closely to your heart, and whose affection and tenderness you hoped might soften the pangs of adversity, and cheer the evening of your life;—tell me for what you would exchange that blessed hope, which after a short interval restores them to you, enrobed in celestial glory, beauty and immortality. Christian! when you have seen the grave close over the mortal remains of the father, who has been your guide and counsellor and the most faithful of friends in your prosperity and adversity; or the kindest of mothers, whose hope and delight you were, who nurtured your helpless infancy, and so often watched while you slept, and so often, by her laborious and affectionate assiduity, soothed the hours of sickness and pain, and who with so many prayers and tears daily approached God's mercy-seat for your health, happiness, improvement and salvation;—tell me for what you would exchange the thrilling hope, that they rest in peace with that divine Father, who cares for them with even more tenderness than they cared for you. Christian! when the bosom friend has been snatched from your side, the friend with whom you took sweet counsel and with whom you walked to the house of God, whose sentiments and sympathies were all yours, whose interests were indissolubly associated with your own; when you have heard the last affectionate farewell, and taken the last look, and caught the last beam of kindness which shot from his closing eyes;—say for what would you exchange the transporting hope of a reunion in purer friendship in a better world.

Christians! (I speak not to the aged only, but to those, who have just passed the morning of life,) when you remark around you the many vacancies which death has made among those whom you loved and valued, when you see how many of the aged and venerable and deep-rooted trees have been upturned, and how many of the fairest opening blossoms nipped, how many in their meridian have been suddenly cut down with the unripe and ungathered fruit hanging thick about them, when you have so often seen death trampling with indifference on the pride and boast of genius, wit and learning, and piercing with his fatal arrow the thickest shield and panoply of virtue, and desolating the fairest scenes of human happiness, usefulness and promise;—tell me have you never felt the infinite value of that hope, which does not permit you to think of them as lost; but which commands you to take a wider prospect of the ways and purposes of God, and remark that some are but transplanted to a more genial soil and clime, there to strike a more vigorous root, to put forth fairer blossoms, and to pour out a sweeter fragrance, and a richer harvest; and that wisdom, benevolence, usefulness, integrity, and piety shall never want scope, and opportunity for exercise, improvement, and progress, so long as the greatest and best of Beings holds the throne of the universe.

GOD OUR FATHER.

Is there a lone and dreary hour,
When worldly pleasures lose their power?
Father! let me turn to thee,
And set each thought of darkness free.

Is there a time of rushing grief,
Which scorns the prospect of relief?
My Father! break the cheerless gloom,
And bid my heart its calm resume.

Is there an hour of peace and joy,
When hope is all my soul's employ?
My Father! still my hopes will roam,
Until they rest with thee, their home.

The noon-tide blaze, the midnight scene,
The dawn, or twilight's sweet serene,
The glow of life, the dying hour,
Shall own my Father's grace and power.

CPSIA information can be obtained
at www.ICGtesting.com
Printed in the USA
LVHW100522120522
718524LV00004B/218

9 783375 001742